in Trouble

THE BOLDS

in Trouble

By Julian Clary

Illustrated by
David Roberts

Andersen Press · London

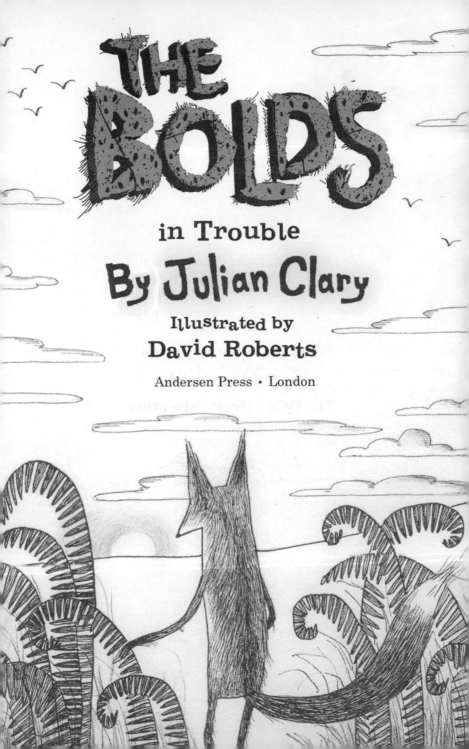

First published in 2018 by

Andersen Press Limited

20 Vauxhall Bridge Road

London SW1V 2SA

www.andersenpress.co.uk

2 4 6 8 10 9 7 5 3 1

British Library Cataloguing in Publication Data available.

Hardback ISBN 978 178 3446 308

Printed and bound in Great Britain by
Clays Limited, Bungay, Suffolk, NR35 1ED

For Joshua
JC

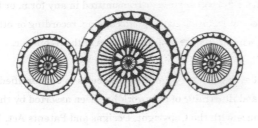

**In memory
of Mickeylove**
DR

Chapter

1

Have you ever had something go **wrong**? You were expecting one thing and then something happened and you ended up getting something else completely different? Well I have, and it can be most upsetting. My mother once made a chocolate cake for tea. I took a bite and spat it out. It tasted horrible!

'Don't be so silly,' said my mother, rather crossly. 'It's a lovely cake. Eat it!' But I couldn't bring myself to. So then she tasted it herself and she couldn't eat it either. 'Something has gone wrong,' she said, pulling a face and gulping down some water to take the awful taste away. Then she looked in the cupboard where she kept the ingredients. Do you know what she'd done? The cocoa powder was in a jar next to the gravy granules and she'd mistakenly picked up the wrong jar. She'd made a gravy cake!

We've been laughing about that mix-up ever since. So you see, sometimes something funny happens by mistake. And sometimes what you think is going to be fun turns out to be the least fun thing ever. Confusing, isn't it? Well that is what this book is about. When things go wrong. Or to be more precise, when things went wrong for the Bolds.

Life was as busy and **eventful** as ever in the Bolds' household.

The Bolds, as you probably know, are a family of hyenas living disguised as human beings in a pleasant tree-lined street called Fairfield Road in Teddington. They wear clothes and hats to cover their hyena features and none

of their human neighbours have guessed their secret, although they *have* noticed that the Bolds seem to laugh an awful lot. Being hyenas, they can't help themselves. They also like to rub their bottoms on tree trunks and bushes to mark their territory, but obviously they can't do that if anyone is watching.

Fred and Amelia Bold are the parents. Fred works at the Christmas cracker factory, writing the silly jokes, and Amelia makes and sells unusual hats at Teddington market. Their children, twins – Bobby and Betty – are lively and funny and sometimes a bit naughty. They go to the local school and are best friends with a girl called Minnie.

Minnie found out about the Bolds' secret a while ago but has promised to tell no one.

Next door lives Nigel McNumpty who, as it turns out, is a grizzly bear. He was grumpy and lonely until the Bolds moved in, but now he's practically one of the  family. He has become best friends with Uncle Tony, an elderly hyena who the Bolds rescued from a local safari park along with Miranda, a sweet little marmoset monkey.

So that's everyone. Except it isn't quite. You see, the Bolds have gained a bit of a reputation for helping other members of the animal world who want to live like humans too. They take in all manner of waifs and strays, teach them how to walk and talk like humans, wear clothes, use a knife and fork and even how to use the toilet. You'd be surprised how many animals there are living amongst us that we fail to notice aren't humans at all. Bus drivers, teachers, athletes, shop assistants . . . prime ministers, even. Only yesterday I had a new sofa delivered by two burly 'men' wearing overalls. They huffed and

puffed and snorted a lot, I noticed. It was only when I spotted their rather moist noses and saw a wisp of steamy sweat rising up in the air from their backs, that I put two and two together. Yes, buffaloes. Brothers, I suspect. I didn't say anything. Buffaloes can be a bit bad-tempered, and I didn't want them to start pawing the ground and charging about. (Not with my new carpet and collection of priceless porcelain dolls I've collected on my travels over the years.) But you see, I knew. And I knew because I have heard about the Bolds.

It wouldn't occur to most people to even think that animals were living in our midst, doing all manner of jobs and, it ought to be said, making an invaluable contribution to society. Only those clever people out there who have read the Bolds books will know to look. Won't we? Have a look around you now. Or if you're on your own, look out of the window. Or if it's dark, turn on the TV. There's one particular newsreader who has all the characteristics of a turtle. Actually, no, don't do that. Reading is much better for you than watching TV. And there's nothing much on these days, is there? But next time you're out and about, see how many 'people' you can spot who you suspect are animals in disguise. Your teacher perhaps? The bus driver? Or maybe the lady who works in the sweet shop?

Probably best not to tell them you've twigged, though. Just give them a knowing look and tap the side of your nose.

But let's get on. Where was I? Ah yes, the Bolds' household. That's all the permanent residents accounted for. But, as I've explained, the Bolds sometimes teach and help animals to make the transition to the human way of life. So when this story begins, there were a few other guests at 41 Fairfield Road whom I really ought to tell you about. The current crop of live-in students at  the Bolds' were a wild boar called Craig, who had trotted all the way to Teddington from a field in Newbury (Craig's ambition was to start his own brewery selling delicious homemade truffle-flavoured alcohol-free beer); Miss Paulina the otter, who didn't have a career in mind, but thought she might have a vocation as a nun. And a very noisy,

rather argumentative goose called Snappy who would one day make a very good traffic warden.

Let's get going. Our story begins with a series of mysterious disappearances. Things start to go missing, and what this leads to is a whole heap of trouble for the Bolds.

One summer's day, before lunchtime, Bobby Bold decided to make himself a cheese sandwich. He buttered two thick slices of bread, piled some cheese and pickle on one, slapped the other slice on top, cut it in half and put it on a plate.

'What else?' he thought. 'Ah, a nice tomato would be tasty.' He turned round to get one from a bowl on the other kitchen counter, rinsed it under the tap and turned back to his sandwich. But would you believe it? The sandwich had gone. Vanished. Just a few crumbs left. He blinked at the empty plate, looked to the left and the right in case he'd moved it, looked over to where the tomatoes were,

but there was no sign of
the cheese sandwich
anywhere. Bobby
scratched his head
and frowned.
Had he eaten it
and forgotten?
His stomach
rumbled loudly,
so he knew that
wasn't it. He
looked around
again, even opening the fridge and
peering inside, just in case he'd put it there.

Some people might have got cross at this
point, but Bobby hardly ever got cross. He
wasn't the type. In fact he smiled.

'Someone is playing a game with me!' he
said to himself. 'Very funny!' He folded his

arms and laughed. 'I know it's you, Betty!' he shouted. 'You can come out now.' But there was no reply. So he opened all the cupboards, fully expecting to find his cheeky twin sister hiding there, but with no results.

'Aha!' he said at last, noticing the back door was open. Bobby wandered into the garden, where Uncle Tony was snoozing in a deckchair and his sister Betty was standing on the patio with her hands on her hips looking crosser than usual.

'Did you drink my lemonade?' she accused her brother. 'I just put it here while I went to get my book and now it's all gone.'

Bobby gasped. 'No way. I was inside making a sandwich, which has also disappeared.'

'Well if it wasn't you, who was it? The only

other person around is Uncle Tony.' The twins looked over to the elderly hyena, dozing in his chair on the lawn.

'He certainly loves sandwiches and lemonade,' agreed Bobby, 'And he's got crumbs on his T-shirt,' he said, getting a little closer.

'He's always got crumbs on his T-shirt,' pointed out Betty, 'but I'm pretty sure he's faking that snoring.'

'Yes, nice one, Tony,' said Bobby. 'You had us going there for a minute.'

But Uncle Tony was deaf as a post these days, and didn't respond. In fact he was snoring quite loudly and appeared to be fast asleep. His mouth was wide open.

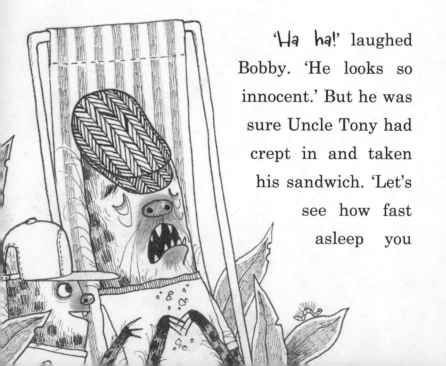

'Ha ha!' laughed Bobby. 'He looks so innocent.' But he was sure Uncle Tony had crept in and taken his sandwich. 'Let's see how fast asleep you really are, shall we?' he chuckled.

'What are you going to do?' asked Betty.

'Wait and see!' said Bobby, laughing wildly as only a hyena can.

Chapter
2

Bobby returned to the kitchen and got a squeezy bottle of mustard from the fridge. He crept back to Uncle Tony, opened the lid, held the mustard upside down over the hyena's open jaws and squeezed: a big dollop of hot mustard drooped down from the bottle like a giant yellow dewdrop. Bobby gave another gentle squeeze.

The dollop trembled for a second before falling silently into Uncle Tony's mouth.

Then Bobby and Betty darted behind a shrub to watch the fun.

At first nothing happened. Then the snoring stopped abruptly and Uncle Tony's nose twitched and his mouth slowly closed.

It occurred to Bobby that, for someone pretending to be asleep, Uncle Tony was being very convincing. Oh dear, what if he *wasn't* the one who'd stolen the sandwich? But it was too late now . . .

Suddenly Uncle Tony's eyes opened. Just a little at first, then wider, wider and WIDER! At the same time, he made a few gentle throat-clearing noises, which quickly gathered momentum until he was coughing and wheezing rather loudly. Eventually a spray of yellow saliva flew across the lawn and poor Uncle Tony staggered out of his deckchair,

his eyes streaming and his nose running as he pawed frantically at his mouth, trying to stop the burning taste. Unable to see properly, he ended up on his arthritic knees crawling, choking and gasping all at once, trying to call for help.

From behind their shrub Betty and Bobby could see that this 'joke' had not been funny at all and had actually gone dangerously wrong. They rushed out to help.

'It's all right, Tony!' shouted Betty, running to turn on the hosepipe. 'Open your mouth and I'll wash it away. Open wide!' She directed the jet of water into Tony's open snout but the poor hyena wasn't expecting that either and hadn't closed his throat. The water went down the wrong hole and only made matters worse. Now he was coughing and gasping for air too.

Hearing the commotion, Mrs Bold rushed out of the house. 'What on earth are you doing

to Tony?' she demanded. She grabbed the hose from her daughter and threw it to one side.

'Tony, Tony!' she said, putting her arm round him and leading him back to the deckchair. 'Just stay calm and try to breathe.'

'W-w-we thought he was playing tricks on us!' said Bobby lamely. 'Oh dear. Is he going to be all right?'

'Get him a glass of water, quickly! And a towel!' said Mrs Bold. Her children ran into the house to do as they were asked.

Slowly Uncle Tony recovered, but he was soaking wet, bewildered and had rivulets of hot yellow stuff running down his face and chest. Mrs Bold wiped his aged grey fur with her pinny and coaxed him into drinking a few sips of water.

'There, there,' she said gently. 'You're all right now, Tony. Calm yourself.'

'Oh my,' said Tony, his voice shaking. 'I was having a lovely nap one minute, then suddenly my mouth was on fire, and it felt like I was underwater. What on earth happened to me?' He peered at Mrs Bold full of bewilderment. 'Was it a bad dream, Amelia?'

'I honestly don't know,' said Mrs Bold. Then she turned to her sheepish-looking children. 'Do you two know what happened?'

'I, well, yes . . .' began Betty.

'We thought he was only pretending to be asleep, that he'd stolen my sandwich and Betty's drink as a joke, so I, er, I—'

'You what?' asked their mother, frowning as

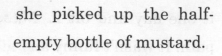

she picked up the half-empty bottle of mustard.

'Put mustard in his mouth,' said Bobby awkwardly. 'It was supposed to be funny. I'm sorry, Tony, really I am.'

'Well it wasn't funny, was it?' said Mrs Bold. 'In fact it was terribly un-funny. I'm surprised at you, Bobby. I really am. And *you*, Betty. Doing something that unkind to an elderly family member.'

Uncle Tony looked up at the twins, bleary-eyed and a little confused. 'You didn't mean to hurt me. I know you'd never do that. It was a joke that went wrong, that's all. When I was a pup in the wild I used to think it was great fun to chase my own tail. Then I caught it one day and bit it. Made myself yelp with pain. It wasn't funny any more and I never did that again. I guess this is a similar thing.'

'Except the children aren't living in the wild,' sniffed Amelia. 'Although they act like it sometimes.'

Mr Bold suddenly appeared at the back door. 'What's going on here? Pups chasing tails? I've got a joke about that.'

Why did the pup chase his tail?

He was trying to make ends meet!

Mrs Bold giggled, although she was trying
to be cross with the children.

What do you do
if a pup eats a
dictionary?

Take the
words out of
his mouth!

Uncle Tony liked this joke and let out a loud,
rather croaky guffaw.

How do you tell the
difference between a pup
and a marine biologist?

One wags a tail, the
other tags a whale!

By now everyone was laughing. The unfortunate incident with the mustard was explained to Mr Bold and then quickly forgotten as the hyenas did what hyenas do best: laughed long and loud until they were all rolling around on their backs on the lawn.

It was some minutes later, during a pause in the hilarity, that a sudden pang of hunger reminded Bobby of something.

'What I don't understand, though,' he said, sitting up and scratching his head, 'is where my sandwich went?'

There was a puzzled silence as all of them pondered this cheesy mystery.

'Well it wasn't any of us,' shrugged Mrs Bold. 'Miranda?'

Uncle Tony shook his head. 'She's fast asleep inside my T-shirt.' Just then a sleepy marmoset monkey popped her head out into the open air.

'What happen? Me dream me on boat. Big storm. Thunderclaps!'

'That was me coughing. Sorry!' said Uncle Tony.

'Ah, poor Tony!' squeaked Miranda. 'You no got coff-coffy?'

'No, my sweet. Just a, er, misunderstanding involving some hot mustard.'

'No coff-coffy no more. Nighty nighty!' said Miranda as she gave a yawn and retreated back inside Uncle Tony's T-shirt to continue her siesta.

'Perhaps it was Mr McNumpty who took my sandwich?' pondered Bobby next, glancing over the fence.

'No. He's gone to the library, I believe,' said his father. 'He's heard there's a book about a bear called Winnie who does a poo somewhere. Something like that anyway.'

'And frankly, he's a bit too big to creep in unnoticed and silently snatch your lunch,' pointed out Mrs Bold.

'Mind if I go back to sleep?' asked Tony, his eyes beginning to droop.

'Of course not, old boy,' said Mr Bold, giving the elderly hyena a pat on the shoulder. 'And the children are very sorry for the mustard business, aren't you?'

The children nodded.

'All forgotten,' said Uncle Tony.

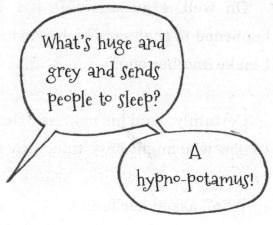

What's huge and grey and sends people to sleep?

A hypno-potamus!

But Uncle Tony didn't hear the punchline. He was fast asleep.

Chapter

The Bolds all wandered back into the house.

'Oh well. I guess we'll never know what happened to that sandwich,' said Bobby. 'Can I make another one?'

'Certainly,' said his mother. 'Though I think I know who might have taken the first one.'

'Who?' asked her family.

'Well, Craig, Miss Paulina and Snappy are in the front room with the dressing-up box, learning about clothes and how to wear them.

Maybe one of *them* got hungry and took your sandwich? They haven't had their manners lessons yet so perhaps they don't know it's wrong to take things without asking.'

In the front room the three students were indeed getting to grips with the tricky business of dressing themselves. It's not as easy as it looks when you haven't done it before and you haven't had a parent or helper to teach you *how* to do it.

Craig the wild boar had squeezed his big barrel chest into a slim-fit coral pink shirt and several of the buttons had burst under the strain. He had a pair of trousers on, but they were inside out and back to front.

Miss Paulina the religious otter had made herself a sort of wimple out of a pair of pastel green shorts, her face was peeking out of one

leg and her hindquarters somehow out of the other. Her ensemble was finished off with a pair of white trainers, the laces of which were still tied together, causing her to fall over, and she lay wriggling on her back trying to get upright again, her big otter tail swishing about frantically.

As for Snappy the goose – well, he'd clearly been pecking furiously at every item he could reach and was sitting in a torn, tattered nest of fabric while other scraps, threads and fragments floated down around him like confetti.

The Bolds entered the lounge and tried not to laugh at the chaotic scene, but they couldn't help themselves.

'Er, how are you getting on?' asked Mrs Bold, covering her snout with both paws.

'I don't think we've quite got the hang of things,' huffed Craig.

'No. You're all . . . pants!' quipped Mr Bold.

'Clothes are stupid, in my opinion,' snapped Snappy. 'Feathers are far more sensible.'

'But humans wear clothes, so you'll have to persevere,' said Mrs Bold.

'I'll help you,' offered Betty.

'Practice makes perfect,' said Miss Paulina with a virtuous smile.

'A good first attempt,' said Mr Bold. 'Now, do any of you know anything about a missing sandwich?' he asked as he and his family helped the students out of what was left of their clothes. 'Only, Bobby made one and then it vanished into thin air before he had a chance to eat it.'

Snappy turned and glared at the Bolds, his beak wide with disbelief. 'Are you calling us thieves?' he said, his long neck jutting forward accusingly. 'The nerve!'

'No, we, er, just wondered, only—'

'Wondered if we accidentally pinched a sandwich? I've never been so insulted in all my days!'

'Please don't get upset, Snappy!' said Bobby. 'We were just trying to solve the mystery.'

'No sandwiches have been eaten by us, more's the pity,' said

Craig, patting his stomach.

'We are innocent of all charges,' added Miss Paulina, nodding in agreement. 'But I will pray for the safe return of your missing lunch.'

The Bolds left them to it and went to the kitchen, where they began making sandwiches for everyone.

As Mr Bold was cutting the cheese, his wife suddenly gripped his arm and sniffed the air.

'I've got it!' she said triumphantly.

'Got what? My sandwich?' asked a confused Bobby.

'No. The culprit. I know who the sandwich thief is! I can smell him!'

Mr Bold put the knife down and sniffed the air too, taking several big, noisy lungfuls.

'Aha!' he said. 'Me too!'

And together they said,

We smell FOX!

Chapter

The Bolds' animal instincts were right. It was indeed a fox who had stolen the sandwich and lemonade, before helping himself to a couple of home-made cupcakes left cooling in the kitchen at Number 45. He then jumped over the fence and took three old chop bones, which he found in a black sack at Number 47. But his daylight raids on the houses of Fairfield Road had not gone unnoticed and there was trouble brewing in that quiet tree-lined street.

A few hours later, Tony was awake after his rest and the twins' best friend Minnie had popped over with her little dog Walter.

Everyone was sitting around the kitchen table enjoying some biscuits and lemon squash, when there was a polite tap on the back door.

'Who's there?' said Mr Bold.

'Rita,' replied a deep voice.

'Rita who?'

'Rita lot of books!' said the deep voice again. Then Mr McNumpty entered, carrying a big pile of books from Teddington library.

'Ha ha!' said Mr Bold. 'That's a good joke. I must remember that and use it in a cracker.'

'Would you like some lemon squash and a biscuit?' asked Mrs Bold.

'Oh yes, rather!' said Mr McNumpty, putting the books on the counter before washing his hands in the kitchen sink.

Why was the biscuit sad?

Because his mummy was a wafer so long!

Once they were all settled and happily chomping on some home-made cookies, the Bolds told their neighbour about the missing cheese sandwich and lemonade, and the joke with the mustard that had gone horribly wrong.

'And then we discovered who the real thief was,' said Mrs Bold. 'Bet you can't guess who.'

'Ah, well, maybe I can,' teased Nigel. 'Was it a fox?'

'How did *you* know?' said Mrs Bold.

'Because I saw one of these in the library,' said Mr McNumpty, pulling a leaflet from his jacket pocket. Betty immediately picked it up and started reading:

ATTENTION

Fairfield Road Residents' Association are calling a meeting tonight at Number 10 Fairfield Road to discuss the alarming problem of urban foxes in our area.

Foxes are entering our homes and gardens day and night in search of food. Something must be done to rid us of these wild, disease-ridden vermin before the problem gets more serious and someone is hurt.

Please come along at 7 p.m. sharp. Soft drinks and nibbles will be provided.

Richard and Zoe Bingham
10 Fairfield Road

'Gosh,' said Mr Bold. 'I don't think the poor foxes are dangerous! Unless you're a cheese sandwich.'

'And I don't think they're disease-ridden, either!' said Mrs Bold indignantly. 'Why do humans always assume that animals are carrying diseases?'

'I don't,' pointed out Minnie. 'You're the cleanest, loveliest friends in the world.'

'Thanks,' said Betty. 'I just don't understand why people think the fox will hurt them. Surely it's the other way round. My teacher says that in the old days people used to hunt foxes.'

'Yes,' said Minnie. 'And there's a stuffed fox in the pub in Broad Street. I saw it when we went out for Mum's birthday. It had glass eyes and a really sad face.'

Mrs Bold shuddered. 'Sometimes I really don't understand human beings. How cruel! Surely that's far worse than a fox who steals the odd sandwich.'

'When we lived in Africa,' said Mr Bold, 'your mother and I were always scavenging in the safari park.'

'Fred . . .' Mrs Bold gave him a warning look.

'Well it's true, my dear. It's what hyenas are famous for – and laughing of course.'

'We've left that life behind us now,' Mrs Bold reminded him.

'Yes I know, but it doesn't mean I'm not sometimes tempted by the delicious smells coming out of dustbins.'

Betty and Bobby giggled – and Minnie pushed her biscuit away, looking a little queasy.

'What I mean,' continued Mr Bold, 'is that I would never condemn an animal for doing what comes naturally to it.'

'But the Binghams seem very upset about the foxes' natural behaviour,' said Minnie.

'They seem to be upset most of the time,' pointed out Mr McNumpty.

The Binghams were known to everyone in Fairfield Road as busybodies. They were a retired couple who seemed to spend most of their (considerable) spare time watching everyone else on the street to make sure they didn't do anything they considered 'wrong'. If your car wasn't parked neatly, they put a note on your windscreen. If children played on the street outside their house, they knocked on the window. And if you didn't trim your hedge, they put a terse letter through your door.

'I think we need to go to this meeting and stick up for the foxes,' said Mr Bold. 'Goodness knows what the Binghams are proposing to do about the 'problem' but I think it's our duty to defend the poor creatures and remind people that animals are not the dangerous ones around here. Why, only yesterday I saw a poor pigeon as flat as a pancake lying in the gutter where it had been squashed by a car. Surely careless driving is far more dangerous than a peckish fox who occasionally helps himself to a snack.'

'Talking of snacks, I wonder what the nibbles will be at this meeting?' pondered Bobby, licking his lips.

'I don't know,' said his mother, 'but *you* won't be trying any. You'll be in bed.'

'Cheesy balls?' said Bobby.

'I beg your pardon?'

'Do you think there'll be cheesy balls? I love them!'

'Then you'll love my new cheese jokes,' said Mr Bold.

'I've got one!' said Bobby, who had inherited his father's love of jokes.

'Go on then, son!' said Mr Bold proudly.

'I know!' jumped in Mr Bold.

'Halloumi!'

Everyone was enjoying the cheesy jokes and had almost forgotten about the foxes.

'It's such fun to have a jolly good laugh,' said Uncle Tony, wiping tears from his bristly cheeks.

'The best things in life are Brie!' said Mr Bold.

Chapter

So that evening Mrs Bold brushed her ears and put on a nice hat, and Mr Bold checked himself for fleas while Uncle Tony got Betty and Bobby ready for bed. Then when the twins were tucked up, their parents went next door to call for Mr McNumpty.

'Now remember,' said their neighbour, 'we need to defend these poor foxes without arousing the local residents' suspicions to the fact that we too are animals. A lovely hat, by the way, Amelia, it covers your ears beautifully.'

'Why thank you,' said Mrs Bold, blushing a little. 'I've gone for a smart but casual look.'

When they arrived at Number 10 they found the house positively heaving. Another neighbour opened the door to them because Mr Bingham was busy trying to find more chairs and Mrs Bingham was repeating for the *sixth* time the terrifying story of finding a fox peering in through her French windows.

'And I said to myself, there and then, Zoe Bingham, it's up to you to do something about this problem before someone really gets hurt.'

The Bolds and Mr McNumpty were ushered into the front room. Mrs Bold found a stool to sit on but Mr Bold and Mr McNumpty had to stand at the back. Mr Bold looked round for the promised nibbles but was rather disappointed: just a single bowl of crisps of indeterminate

flavour and some rubbery carrot crudités with a beige dip that might have been hummus (but not from one of the better supermarkets) served on a chipped saucer. Furthermore, the meeting was so well attended, these sparse offerings were gobbled up in no time. Mr Bold thought about licking the bowl the crisps had been in, but decided he'd better not and made do with his watery beaker of squash. But the poor standard of the refreshments was soon forgotten once the heated debate got under way.

'Foxes are everywhere. We must do something!' declared Mr Bingham ominously, before Mrs Bingham told again the story of the fox peering in at her French windows.

And the rest of the neighbours seemed to be in agreement that the foxes were a nuisance.

Shoot them, I say!

Vermin!

It was all getting very animated and the neighbours were clearly all of one mind: the foxes **must** be got rid of. Mr and Mrs Bold were conspicuous by their silence. Eventually Zoe Bingham turned to Amelia Bold.

'Well, what do *you* think? Have you been invaded yet?'

'Well, I rather like foxes,' said Mrs Bold.

The room suddenly fell silent.

'You like them?!'

'Er, yes. Beautiful creatures,' continued Amelia. 'And I don't see why we can't all get along together perfectly well.'

There was a collective gasp. Mrs Bold looked to her husband for support. Mr Bold looked rather blank for a moment, and then his eyes lit up.

What did the grape say when the fox trod on it?

Nothing. He just let out a little wine!

Several neighbours tutted disapprovingly and exchanged glances with each other.

'My husband works in the Christmas cracker factory,' explained Mrs Bold. 'He writes the jokes . . .'

'Good for him,' sniffed Richard Bingham. 'But I find it hard to believe that your house is the only one that hasn't been affected by these wretched foxes. Something must be done!'

'Well there are natural ways to deter foxes,' said Mrs Bold.

'Yes,' said Mr McNumpty. 'I read in the library that they don't like male urine. Perhaps you could wee round your garden to stop the foxes coming in.'

'Do what round our garden?' fumed Mr Bingham. 'I've never heard anything so disgusting.'

'Lion poo,' shouted someone else.

'I beg your pardon?'

'Lion poo. Apparently foxes hate lion poo. Let's get some of that.'

(That's actually true, by the way. I know it sounds crazy but look it up if you don't believe me!)

'Where on earth are we going to get lion poo from?' laughed Mrs Bingham in an unpleasant way. 'This is Teddington, not Africa.'

'You could try London Zoo,' suggested Mr Bold.

Mrs Bingham shuddered. 'Really. If that's

the best solution you can come up with, then I think it's probably better if you keep your solutions to yourself. These foxes need to be got rid of – we're not going to achieve that by weeing and pooing in our back gardens!'

'Animals and humans can live together perfectly well, so long as we are considerate and respectful,' stated Mr McNumpty. 'I expect the foxes have lived here a lot longer than we have.'

'But they should live in the countryside. Not here in Teddington.'

'Why should they?' said Mr McNumpty. 'Who says?'

'I say!' said Richard Bingham, getting rather red in the face.

This set everyone off again and the room
was very quickly in uproar.

Mrs Bold and Mr McNumpty tried to argue that *no* children had been bitten, nor would they be, and that foxes are generally clean animals. But no one could hear them. Mr Bold had several more foxy jokes up his sleeve but *he* couldn't be heard either.

In the end there was nothing Mr and Mrs Bold or Mr McNumpty could say to change anyone's opinion and it was decided that a private pest control company called 'POW TO PESTS!' should be contacted. They would catch the foxes in a trap and then drive them out to the middle of nowhere and let them go.

'But won't they just find their way back?' asked one lady. 'My dog found his way back from Guildford when we left him at my mother's.'

'Well that's why I'm suggesting we use POW,' said Mr Bingham. 'I have it on good authority (although they'll never admit it) that the foxes aren't really "let go". They're "dealt with" in the countryside.'

'What do you mean?' asked Mrs Bold.

'I mean they go to fox heaven!'

Mrs Bold looked confused.

'They kill them,' said Mrs Bingham bluntly. 'In a very humane way,' she added. 'I don't suppose they feel a thing.'

'Well we don't know that for certain,' said Mr Bingham. 'But suffice to say this company gives a one hundred per cent guarantee that the foxes won't return.'

'But that's murder,' said Mr Bold. 'You can't do that.'

'We can and we will. All those in favour of using POW to rid us of this problem, raise your hands.'

Every hand in the room went up, except the paws of Mr Bold, Mrs Bold and Mr McNumpty.

Chapter

By the time they got home, Mrs Bold was crying and Mr Bold had lost the desire to tell any jokes.

'Oh dear,' said Uncle Tony when he saw everyone's faces. 'It didn't go well then?'

'It was awful,' said Mrs Bold, blowing her snout loudly into a handkerchief. 'They want to catch those poor foxes in a cage and take them away . . .'

'To be killed,' added Mr McNumpty.

'Oh, poor foxy!' cried Miranda. 'They no deservey that.'

'I know,' agreed Mr Bold. He was feeling rather guilty. 'I have to admit I've been down the odd bin myself when no one was looking. Found half a pizza the other week, in the one at Number 15. I could smell it from here. Still warm, it was!'

'It would have been a terrible waste. You did the right thing,' agreed Uncle Tony.

'But now a fox has probably got the blame,' said Bobby, who was listening at the door with his sister.

'What are you two doing up?' asked his mother.

'We couldn't sleep. We wanted to hear about the meeting.'

'Well it's not something I want you hearing about.'

'Too late, Mum, we've already heard. The foxes are in grave danger.'

'We've got to do something,' said Betty.

'We warn foxy!' piped up Miranda from her spot on the windowsill. 'Tell foxy be careful. Peeps out to get them!'

'That,' said Mr Bold, 'is an excellent idea, Miranda.'

'You welcome,' said Miranda.

'We can speak to the foxes, animal to animal, and tell them the danger they're facing. But we'd better act quickly. The pest control van will probably be here tomorrow. Those Binghams don't want to waste any time,' added Mrs Bold.

'But how do we contact the foxes?' asked Bobby.

'We go to Bushy Park,' said Uncle Tony. 'I've definitely smelled fox when I've taken a stroll through the park. There's a distinct aroma near the ice-cream van. If those ones aren't the culprits we can at least get a message to them through one of their clan.'

'Right,' said Mr Bold looking at the clock on the mantelpiece. 'The park. Of course. It's nearly nine o'clock now. It will soon be getting dark . . .'

'Foxy come out at dusk,' offered Miranda.

'Or any time they're peckish,' corrected Bobby. 'It was just before lunchtime when my sandwich went missing.'

'We need to be careful, though,' warned Mr McNumpty. 'If our neighbours see us having a cheery chat with a fox, their suspicions will be aroused. The last thing we need is people suspecting we're animals and capturing us too.'

'Very true,' said Uncle Tony. 'Very true.'

'This will have to be an undercover operation,' concluded Mr McNumpty. 'We will have to creep into the park at midnight, once everyone else is safely tucked up in bed.'

'That's rather late for the twins,' cautioned Mrs Bold.

'Please let us come,' said Betty. 'We promise to be good.'

'Come on, Dad,' said Bobby. 'We've been on all your adventures before. We won't be able to sleep anyway, knowing you're out there trying to help other animals.'

'What do you think, Fred?' said Mrs Bold.

'Well. This is an emergency. The future of these foxes is at stake. I think under the circumstances we'd better let the twins come with us.'

'Very well, Bobby and Betty,' said Mrs Bold. 'You may come too. It's Sunday tomorrow, so at least you'll be able to sleep in.'

What nice parents animals are. Most human parents would have said: 'Absolutely not. Wandering round the park at midnight? No way. Go to bed.' Bobby and Betty were very lucky pups.

'There's just one problem,' said Mr McNumpty, rubbing his chin. 'The park is closed at night. The gates will be locked.'

'Hmmm,' said Mr Bold. 'Hadn't thought of that.'

'Well,' reasoned Bobby. 'If the foxes can get out, we must be able to get in.'

'Maybe there's a hole?' suggested Mrs Bold. 'We'll find a way through, I'm sure.'

'Could we dig?' suggested Betty.

'Or take the students with us,' said Bobby. '*They* could help. Craig is very strong and Miss Paulina has sharp teeth.'

'I don't think so,' said Mrs Bold. 'They're not ready for such a serious excursion. They still can't dress themselves and they might give the game away. Leave them here asleep.'

'Come on then, let's all try to get a little sleep before our mission begins,' said Mr Bold. 'We will leave for the park at midnight. These foxes need our help. We'll find a way in.'

Chapter

So later that night, when all the lights in all the houses in Fairfield Road were out, the Bold family and Mr McNumpty quietly left Number 41 and crept along to the gates of Bushy Park.

But how were they going to get over the wall? There was no sign of a hole. It looked like they would have to start digging, which Mr Bold worried would take too long and might alert someone to what they were doing. But as it happens, Mrs Bold had rather cleverly decided to wear one of her unusual hats and this one was made of old bed springs, just in case they were needed. And of course they were.

'My dear, you're a genius!' declared Mr Bold.
'We'll tie them to our feet and bounce over the
wall!' And so they did – one by one. There were
some mishaps, of course, where they didn't
quite bounce high enough and hit the wall, but
after much stifled laughter and some trial
and error, the whole party finally made
it into the park.

It was pitch black but
luckily hyenas can
see in the dark.

'This way,' said Betty. 'Follow me,' and she led the others to an area of the park that was quite wild and overgrown with brambles and ferns.

'They should be around here somewhere,' she said, peering into the darkness. They all waited for a while, but there was only silence and the odd hoot of an owl watching from the trees above.

Then Mr McNumpty spotted two sly eyes peering at them from several yards away.

'Yoo hoo!' he called. 'Mr Fox? Mrs Fox? Do you think we might have a word? It's rather urgent. Don't worry, we're not really humans. We're animals in disguise. I'm actually a grizzly bear and my friends here are hyenas.'

Now you might think it unlikely that a

grizzly bear could speak to a fox and expect any kind of answer, but there is a simple explanation: all animals can understand each other. What sounds to us like incomprehensible barks, growls, purrs or squawks are all crystal clear if you're an animal, of whatever species. Thus a zebra can speak to a sparrow, a shark can chat with a salmon, a monkey can gossip with a caterpillar and so on. It's one of the marvels of the animal kingdom that the BBC has yet to do a programme about.

So it was therefore a surprise to Mr McNumpty when there was no answer. The eyes stared at him without blinking and then disappeared. And a rather pungent aroma seemed to float closer and get up everyone's nostrils.

'Oh!' said Mr McNumpty. 'That's strange . . .'

'Let me try,' said Mrs Bold, and she cleared her throat.

'Mr Fox? I know you're here somewhere. We don't mean to frighten you. Forgive us for calling on you uninvited, but there's something we think you ought to know. You see, we live in Fairfied Road and – ouch!' A sharp pain struck the back of Amelia's hind leg.

'Ow!' cried out Bobby, spinning round.

'Aaagh!' shrieked Betty.

'Ooh!' exclaimed Mr Bold.

Everyone, it seemed, was being nipped on their ankles, one after the other, apart from Miranda, who was perched safely on Uncle Tony's shoulder. Mr McNumpty was probably bitten too, but his fur was so thick he didn't notice. Everyone else was hopping about clutching their legs and wondering what on earth was going on, when an unfamiliar voice – rough and angry – hissed: 'Now clear off and don't come back or I'll bite you properly next time!'

There was a rustling of ferns behind them and the sound of whoever it was stealthily running away.

'Everyone all right?' asked a concerned Mr McNumpty.

'Betty? Bobby? Come here, dears. Let's have a look at your legs. Teeth marks! What a horrid fox!'

As the attacker had said, they weren't 'proper' bite marks – no blood had been drawn – just warning nips. But it was a shock nevertheless.

'But we were only trying to help!' cried Betty.

'To save him from the pest control people!' Bobby pointed out. The twins were both tired and upset with the way the mission to help a fellow animal had turned out.

'Foxy no nicey,' said Miranda, shaking her head.

'No. Not nice at all,' agreed Uncle Tony. 'I shall probably have a noticeable limp for several days.'

'Come on, everyone,' said Mrs Bold. 'Let's get home before he bites us again. We're not going to be able to warn him after all.'

'Good riddance,' muttered Mr McNumpty.

It was very late when the Bolds got home after this unsuccessful trip to Bushy Park. They were all a little out of sorts, not to mention tired, so the twins were given a drink of milk and then everyone went straight to bed.

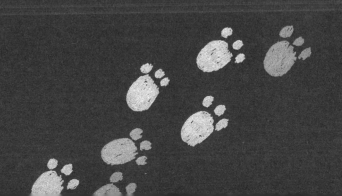

Chapter

8

The Bolds were all still feeling a little sorry
for themselves the next morning over a rather
late breakfast, when Minnie came to visit with
Walter, whom she'd been taking for a walk.
I say walk, but Walter didn't like to walk
more than a few metres. He liked to be carried,
preferably tucked inside
Minnie's fleece, which
is where he was this
morning.

The twins told
Minnie about the
late-night trip

to help the foxes and the rather unpleasant welcome they'd received.

'Gosh,' said Minnie. 'What a bad-tempered old fox.'

'But the worst of it is,' said Betty, rubbing her ankle, 'we didn't get to tell him about the pest control van.'

'He wouldn't listen!' said Bobby. 'He still doesn't know the danger he's facing.'

'Oh don't bother about him,' said Snappy the goose, who had been trying for several minutes to get some marmalade out of the jar with his beak. 'Foxes get all they deserve. I have no sympathy for them.'

'That's not very kind,' said Miss Paulina.

'Well it's true. My grandfather was killed by a fox, and so were two of my aunts. It's about time they got a taste of their own medicine. The humans are talking sense on this. I'm glad I'm going to be a human.'

Mrs Bold raised her eyes and Mr Bold shook his head.

'I once heard a wonderful story about a fox and a goose and the power of prayer,' said Miss Paulina.

'Not now,' said Craig the wild boar, who was feeling rather bad-tempered over not being invited to the park the night before.

Minnie thought for a moment. 'Well from the sound of it, there's only one thing that interests this fox.'

'What's that?' asked Mrs Bold.

'Food!' said Minnie. 'Did you take along a few tasty treats?'

'No,' shrugged Mrs Bold.

'Well look at it from the fox's point of view,' said Minnie. 'You crept onto his home turf in the dead of night. That frightened him for starters. He probably thought you were trying to trick him. Catch him, even. He knows foxes are not very liked around here. If you'd offered him some food he might have stayed around to listen to what you had to say.'

'Good point!' said Mr Bold. 'I know he likes cheese sandwiches, so let's take him some of those! I'll start making some right away.'

'The other thing is . . . How can I put it?' added Minnie, looking awkward.

'What? Out with it!' encouraged Mr McNumpty.

'Well. Foxes have a very good sense of smell, don't they?' began Minnie.

'So do we,' interrupted Mrs Bold. 'We are hyenas after all.'

'Well exactly. He'd have smelled you, you see. And Mr McNumpty. You might all be dressed as humans, look like humans and sound like humans, but to a fox's sensitive nose you're still a bunch of hyenas, a grizzly bear and a marmoset monkey! That must have been rather alarming and confusing for him.'

'Can't do much about that, can we?' said a slightly offended Betty, giving her armpit a suspicious sniff.

'Are you saying we're all a bit **whiffy**?' said Mrs Bold, just as indignantly.

'No, not to me,' Minnie replied hastily. 'But maybe to a fox you are.'

Mr Bold decided it was time for a joke.

What did the left eye say to the right eye?

Between you and me, something smells!

Everyone enjoyed this joke, so he tried another.

How many skunks does it take to make a big stink?

Quite a phew!

'I think our hyena smell is very nice,' said Bobby.

'Well, I think my grizzly smell is very attractive too,' said Mr McNumpty. 'But I take Minnie's point. Maybe we didn't think through our visit to the foxes properly.'

'So to sum up,' said Mrs Bold, jumping in before her husband told more jokes and everyone forgot about the problem in hand,

'Dangerous as it is, we should have gone in daylight; we need to take sandwiches; and we should all have a good scrub in the bath. And I've got some perfume we can all have a generous squirt of before we go.'

'What's it called?' asked Bobby suspiciously.

'Well, your father bought it for my birthday. It's called An Evening in Paris.'

'Eew!' responded Bobby. 'I'm not spraying myself with that!'

'Well your mother bought me some aftershave. You can use that instead,' said Mr Bold.

'And what's that called?' Betty asked.

'An Afternoon in Hampton Wick.'

'Right then, twins. That's enough talk. Upstairs to the bath, please,' said Mrs Bold.

What bird steals soap from the bath?

Robber ducks!

Several hours later, after everyone had bathed and scrubbed and perfumed themselves, and Mr Bold had made plenty of cheese sandwiches, they set off, much like any other family going for an outing to the park. As it was a hot summer's day, Mrs Bold wore one of her own hats – a large white umbrella-like arrangement, with garlands of flowers draped around it and several life-like pigeons perched on top.

When they got to the area where the foxes lived, they spread out the picnic blanket and placed the sandwiches and some cakes enticingly on it, then retreated a few yards to watch. They were anxious that no one saw them. They certainly didn't want to draw attention to themselves or be seen talking to a fox, so they moved as far away as possible from other people, and Miranda kept watch up in a tree.

They didn't have to wait long. Within a minute a furry snout emerged from the ferns, twitching with interest. The large, well-fed fox then glided into view and headed straight for the Bolds' sandwiches. He had a quick sniff and then began to gulp them down.

'Ah, hello there!' said Mrs Bold cautiously. 'We thought you might like a cheese sandwich. Don't mind us . . .'

The fox stared coldly at Mrs Bold, then at Mr Bold, Bobby and Betty, Uncle Tony and Miranda, Mr McNumpty and finally Minnie. Walter gave a little whimper and retreated inside Minnie's fleece.

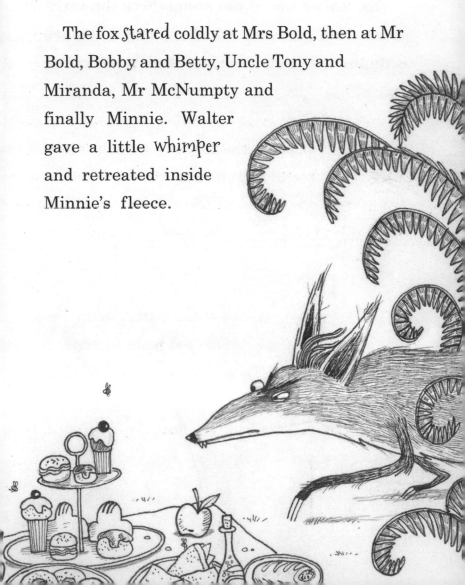

The fox's eyes narrowed and he curled his lip, revealing a row of sharp white teeth.

'Er, we're the Bolds,' said Fred brightly. 'From Number 41 Fairfield Road. We're animals too, well, most of us are. What's your name?'

'Mossy,' grunted the fox, his mouth full of wholemeal bread and cheddar cheese. Then he

looked behind him, towards the ferns and gave a gruff call.

Another slimmer, more-elegant fox obeyed his call, and although startled by the audience, nevertheless approached the picnic blanket and delicately helped herself to a sandwich.

'She's Sylvie,' said Mossy, nodding his head in the direction of the female fox. 'Whaddya want? Hurry up!'

'Pleased to meet you both,' said Mrs Bold. 'We've come to warn you. You've upset some of the people in Fairfield Road.'

'Ha!' said Mossy, unconcerned and pausing to spit out a piece of pickle that wasn't to his liking. 'Good!'

But Sylvie seemed to understand, and

nodded at Mrs Bold to continue. 'Is it the stealing?' she asked quietly. 'I've tried to tell Mossy.' She glanced at the bigger fox, but he rolled his eyes.

'She's right, Mossy,' said Mr McNumpty. 'We're animals too, and we understand the need to find food wherever you can, but you've overstepped the mark.'

'Oh really?' said Mossy, sitting back on his haunches for a moment as he contemplated a French fancy. 'How's that then?'

'Going down bins is one thing. We've all done it.'

'Well I certainly haven't!' said Minnie.

'No, well, most of us have. But you've got too brazen, Mossy. Too greedy. You've been going into people's houses, taking food from their tables!'

'Digging up vegetables!' said Uncle Tony.

'Going through cat flaps!' said Bobby.

'In broad daylight!' said Betty.

'And now the humans are going to do something about it,' said Mr Bold.

Mossy flicked a fly away from his ear and began to eat his second cake. 'I'm shaking from head to paw, really I am,' he said sarcastically. 'Now let me guess . . . Are they going to store the food away in Tupperware boxes? Lock the cat flap? Stay up all night waiting for me with a catapult?'

'No it's far worse than that,' said Mrs Bold.

'Oh, horror of horrors, are they sending for the pest control van? A couple of silly old fools in nylon overalls that will set a trap baited with a spoonful of cheap cat food and expect me to fall for it? Don't make me laugh!'

'I don't think you realise the danger you're in. Or the danger you're putting Sylvie in,' said Mr McNumpty gravely. 'This is serious.'

'Perhaps we should listen to them,' said Sylvie, looking pleadingly at her fellow fox. 'They've come here to help us. And they are the Bolds. Famous for helping animals everywhere.'

'Shut up whining at me, vixen!' said Mossy, wiping his snout on the picnic blanket and belching loudly. 'Yes, I've heard of you Bolds. Everyone has heard of you. But do you want to know something? I think you're a disgrace to your own kind.'

The Bolds all looked at each other in astonishment. Wherever they went animals usually thanked them, admired how they had made a new life for themselves or at the very

least gave them a conspiratorial wink. They'd
never had a reaction like Mossy's before.

'Why do you say that?' asked Mr Bold.

'Just look at you all for a start: dressed up,
teetering around on your hind legs reeking
of some awful perfume that I wouldn't use
to freshen up my toilet. If I had one. Your
relatives in Africa would wee themselves
laughing if they could see what you've become,'
sneered Mossy. 'Namby-pamby, middle-class
yapping yuppies.'

'Oh I say!' said Mrs Bold. 'Really!'

'Did I ask you to come round here sticking
your snout into our business? No I didn't!'
Mossy was getting worked up now. He stood,
then paced menacingly towards the Bolds.
Mrs Bold pushed the twins behind her, and Mr

McNumpty stood forward, ready to protect his friends should things turn nasty.

'I'm not going to hurt you,' taunted Mossy 'I wouldn't waste my energy.'

'We've just come to warn you, that's all,' said Uncle Tony reasonably. 'Hunt a bit more. Scavenge. Eat slugs and birds like country foxes do. Then no one will mind you being here.'

'It might be healthier for us, too,' agreed Sylvie, glancing at Mossy's big stomach. Mossy shot her a warning glare.

'Why go to all that bother?' he sneered. 'There's far tastier food for the taking in Fairfield Road. I had a nice pork chop for my breakfast, conveniently left on the kitchen counter at Number 28 with the back door wide open.' He rubbed his tummy at the memory.

'And a pint of milk from the doorstep at Number 14 washed it down nicely.'

'You a thief! People no likey!' said Miranda bravely, from the safety of Uncle Tony's shoulder.

Mossy leered at the monkey as if she might make a tasty snack one day.

'She's right, though,' pleaded Sylvie. 'We'll pay for all this stolen food one day. The humans might trap us and send us far away. Somewhere awful. Like Chatham.'

'We're foxes, remember?' Mossy said to Sylvie. He shook his mane of dark red fur and looked proud and regal. 'We're not pretending to be something we're not, like this lot. So *what* if people don't like us and are coming to hunt us down? That's always been the case. People don't like foxes and they never have. Nothing is going to change that. But we can outfox the lot of them. Just you see.'

'But if they catch you we think they're planning to kill you,' warned Mrs Bold.

Sylvie's eyes widened in shock.

'No surprise there,' said Mossy. 'Humans love killing foxes. Both my grannies were killed in fox hunts and my uncle escaped one but was never the same afterwards. Went mad, he did. We'll just have to make sure we don't get caught then, won't we?'

'Is there nothing we can say to change your mind?' asked Mrs Bold.

'Nope,' said Mossy. 'Thank you for the sandwiches and the cakes. Very considerate of you. I'm almost sorry I bit your ankles last night.' He laughed quietly to himself. 'But not quite. Say goodbye to the Bolds and their friends,' he instructed Sylvie.

Sylvie looked sadly at the visitors and shrugged. 'Goodbye. And thank you for the warning. We will be extra careful from now on.'

'Let's go,' Mossy commanded gruffly. 'Those raspberries in the allotments should be ripe by now.'

And with that, they disappeared silently into the ferns, just the occasional quiver in the greenery revealing their route.

Chapter

After all the unpleasantness from Mossy, everyone agreed they needed cheering up, so a visit to the swings was agreed upon.

As they walked across the park, Mr Bold made everyone laugh with some jokes.

Why did the chicken cross the playground?

To get to the other slide!

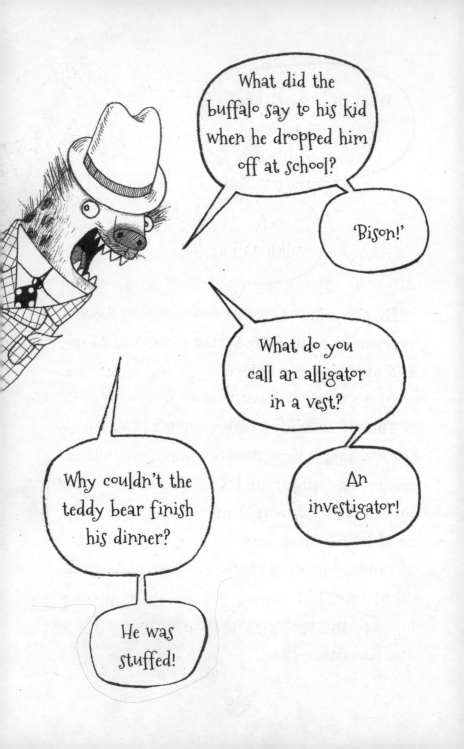

What do you get when you cross a parrot with a centipede?

A walkie-talkie!

By the time they reached the playground, everyone was in a far better mood and Mossy and his nasty remarks were almost forgotten.

The twins had a rather vigorous game on the see-saw, where they bounced up in the air rather alarmingly and Mrs Bold had to tell them to calm down. Minnie and Walter went on the slide over and over again and so did Miranda, who didn't bother going up the stairs each time, but leaped up the slide instead, much to the amazement of the other children and parents.

Mr and Mrs Bold really wanted to join in and were itching to go on the swings, but there was a big sign saying the facilities were only for children aged twelve or under. Instead they 'helped' the twins on the see-saw, one either end, catching them after they flew up in the air, and laughed and whooped as if they were children themselves.

'I wonder what will happen to those foxes?' pondered Uncle Tony as he and Mr McNumpty enjoyed an ice cream each, watching the fun from a bench.

Mr McNumpty shook his head. 'I have a rather bad feeling about it. We've tried to help them. Told them about the danger they're in. But they won't listen. I don't know what else we can do,' he sighed.

'When I was a pup back in Africa,' remembered Tony, 'my mother told me not to eat the berries that grew on a certain bush in the rainy season. But they were big and juicy and looked delicious. I was hungry one day, and decided that just one or two wouldn't do me any harm. So I ate them.'

'No!' gasped Mr McNumpty. 'What happened?'

'I turned green, apparently,' said Uncle Tony, shuddering at the memory. 'I was sick for a week. Both ends . . .'

'I expect you listened to your mother after that?' chuckled Mr McNumpty.

Tony nodded. 'I certainly did. But I wish I'd listened to her before.'

The old friends sat in silence while they contemplated what the future might hold for the two foxes. As things turned out, they were not going to have to wait long to find out.

Over the next few days there were more incidents of theft and vandalism in Fairfield Road, and the residents were outraged. POW TO PESTS couldn't come until Friday and in

that time Mossy seemed to be getting more and more daring in his raids. Something crept up on a schoolgirl one morning as she waited for the bus and raided her satchel, silently making off with her lunchbox before she noticed. A man eating a kebab outside a pub one evening had it snatched from his hand by what he described as 'a flash of fangs and fur'. And a birthday celebration barbecue was in ruins after the cool box containing all the meat and sausages was dragged into the undergrowth, when the cook wasn't looking, and emptied of its entire contents. They had to make do with salad and a French stick, which wasn't much of a party. The local paper ran a front-page headline: **FOX FURY IN FAIRFIELD ROAD** and Mr and Mrs Bingham urged POW to come as soon as they could.

Rumour had it that Mr Bingham was actually seen desperately urinating all round his garden one night – but I don't know for sure and he denied ever doing such a vulgar thing, apart from in his toilet obviously.

Finally POW arrived on the scene and their sinister pest control vans were soon patrolling the streets of Teddington. Large metal cage traps were set in several gardens in Fairfield Road and baited with pet food. Once a fox was trapped, it would be driven miles and miles away, into the countryside to meet its fate.

The Bolds could do nothing but watch in horror.

'Mossy said they wouldn't fall for anything so simple, didn't he?' asked a worried Betty.

'Yes, dear. He did,' said Mrs Bold.

'I know he's not very nice, but no animal deserves to be caught like that, does it?' said Bobby.

'No, son,' agreed Mr Bold. 'He might be rather rude but he's still a living creature and I would do anything to save him.'

'And what about Sylvie?' asked Betty. 'She seems really nice. What if she falls for the bait and gets trapped?' She began to cry.

'There, there,' said her mother. 'We'll think of something. We won't let those cruel humans hurt fellow animals.'

But it seemed that maybe Mossy was right and the pest control people really were nothing for him to worry about. Several days passed, and according to the gossip on Fairfield Road not a single fox had been caught.

'Not so much as a fieldmouse!' huffed Zoe Bingham when she and her husband bumped into Mr Bold on Teddington High Street. 'The traps are useless and the thefts are still continuing. Why, a fox even had the cheek to wee in my garden when I had my nice clean washing hanging out.'

'Are you sure it was a fox?' said Mr Bold, giving Mr Bingham a wink.

Mr Bingham blushed. 'I think we're going to try some different bait tonight,' he said, changing the subject. 'I hear this fox likes cheese.'

'Oh no, foxes hate cheese,' said Mr Bold hurriedly. 'Never touch the stuff.'

'That's not what I heard,' said Zoe through pursed lips, and she stalked off, her husband running behind to catch up.

Chapter

It seems though that the change in bait had an effect because that very night something happened. It was a wet, thundery night and everyone was fast asleep in the Bolds' household when a frantic scratching and high-pitched whining was heard at the kitchen window. Miranda the marmoset monkey noticed it first. She was a light sleeper anyway, and that night had curled up on the stairs to sleep. She crept into the kitchen and saw paws banging on the glass and heard urgent, pitiful crying. She quickly leaped up the stairs and onto Mr and Mrs Bold's bed where she prodded them both awake.

'Scratchy knocky knocky in kitchen! You come quick!' she cried in her high-pitched monkey voice. 'Someone in trouble!'

'Oh dear, Miranda!' said Mrs Bold, reaching for her dressing gown. 'It's the middle of the night!'

'I'll go first,' said Mr Bold gallantly. 'That reminds me . . .'

What woke the ghost up in the middle of the night?

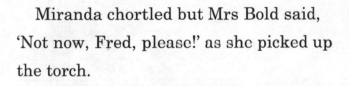

Coffin!

Miranda chortled but Mrs Bold said, 'Not now, Fred, please!' as she picked up the torch.

Down in the kitchen the scratching was even more frantic, the paws just a blur through the glass.

'What IS it?' asked Mrs Bold, shining the beam of the torch towards the source of the noise.

'Me *scaredy!*' said Miranda, jumping on top of the fridge for safety.

'Who's there?' asked Mrs Bold.

'Ice cream,' answered Mr Bold.

Ice cream who?

I scream every time I see a ghost!

Suddenly the scratching stopped and a pair of large desperate amber eyes peered through the kitchen window.

'Mr Bold?' said an agitated voice.

'Quick, open the door, Fred,' said Mrs Bold. 'I think it's Sylvie.'

'Hold on, my dear!' called Fred, as he slid open the bolt and turned the key. At last the door was opened and a panting Sylvie flung herself on the doormat. She was covered in mud, and soaked to the skin, and there were several bloody gashes on her face.

'Oh, poor Sylvie!' said Mrs Bold. 'Come inside quickly. Whatever have you done to yourself?' She reached for a tea towel and began to gently wipe the mud from Sylvie's fur.

Just then the kitchen door swung open again, and there was Mr McNumpty from next door, dressed in striped pyjamas and a tartan dressing gown with matching nightcap.

'What's all the commotion?' he asked.

'It's Sylvie,' said Mrs Bold. 'Something has happened.'

'You've got to help me,' said the fox. 'Mossy's been caught in a cage trap.'

'Oh nooo! Foxy twappy!' wailed Miranda.

'This is very bad news,' said Mr McNumpty.

'Don't worry, Sylvie. We'll help,' said Mr Bold, patting the bedraggled fox on the shoulder. 'Where is he?'

'In the back garden at Number 10. I've been trying to chew my way through the wire, but it's no good. And Mossy . . . He's raging. Screeching and . . .' She couldn't go on.

'Don't worry. We'll go there and unlock the door. He'll be free in no time,' said Fred. But Sylvie shook her head.

'It's not that simple. Those humans who live at Number 10—'

'Richard and Zoe?' offered Mr McNumpty. 'Dreadful couple.'

'Whatever their names are. They've been watching through the window. They're thrilled

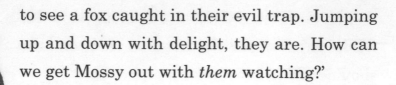

to see a fox caught in their evil trap. Jumping up and down with delight, they are. How can we get Mossy out with *them* watching?'

'But it's three o'clock in the morning!' said Mrs Bold. 'No one will see us.'

'They'll be on guard until the pest control people come to take him away in the morning, for sure. I heard them say as much. The man said he was going to make some strong coffee so that they stay awake.'

'Well we could follow the van in our little Honda, watch where they take Mossy in the countryside and rescue him,' offered Mr Bold.

'We might lose him on the way,' Amelia pointed out. 'And arrive too late.'

'Please hurry,' said Sylvie, her voice

cracking with emotion. 'There must be something we can do.'

There was a thoughtful silence.

'I have an idea!' said Mr McNumpty suddenly.

'Really?' said Sylvie, a glimmer of hope in her eyes.

'Yes. It's a long shot, but it just might work. Miranda? You go and wake everyone up. And I mean everyone. The students too. For this we're going to need all hands on deck.'

'What is the plan?' asked Mr Bold.

'I'll tell you in a minute. Meanwhile you and Mrs Bold must take your clothes off.'

'Nigel!' said Mrs Bold, aghast.

'Just do as I ask please,' said Mr McNumpty firmly. 'If this is going to work everyone must follow my instructions exactly.'

By then a bleary-eyed Uncle Tony, Bobby, Betty, Craig, Miss Paulina and Snappy had

gathered in the kitchen, yawning.

'Listen up, everyone,' said Mr McNumpty, sounding like a stern sergeant major in charge of his fearless troops. 'It's now half past three in the morning. We don't have much time. Here's my plan . . .'

Can you guess what Mr McNumpty's plan was? I'll give you a clue. What are Richard and Zoe most afraid of? Foxes? But more than that – WILDLIFE! Anything that might disturb their neat suburban lifestyle. So what might distract them from guarding Mossy long enough for the Bolds to rescue him? Yes. LOTS AND LOTS OF WILDLIFE! I think I've said enough, don't you? I don't want to spoil the excitement of what's to come. And come it will. On the next few pages . . .

Sylvie was too traumatised to contribute to the rescue plan, Mr McNumpty decided, and he told Uncle Tony that it was his job to remain at Number 41 to look after her.

'Some sweet milky tea might be in order,' he instructed his friend.

'As for the rest of you, this is Operation Free Mossy. Mossy is currently trapped in a cage in the garden of Number 10. Mr and Mrs Bingham are situated at the rear of the property, drinking coffee by the French windows. Our strategy is to distract them and give them reason to move from this vantage point so we can liberate Mossy.

'I envisage a three-pronged attack. Snappy, Craig and Miss Paulina, you are first in: Bait and Distraction. Mr and Mrs Bold, you are Espionage and Counter-attack. Bobby and Betty, you are Raid and Seize. When I give the command, you approach the cage, release the door and guide Mossy to the safety of the kitchen at Number 41. Then the operation will be complete. Are there any questions?'

It was all getting a little serious for Mr Bold and I'm afraid he couldn't resist.

What has four legs and goes 'boo'?

A cow with a cold!

'Mr Bold!' shouted Mr McNumpty. 'Behave yourself please! This, may I remind you, is not a laughing matter.'

Chapter

So here is what happened.

Richard and Zoe Bingham were sitting in their nightclothes by the French windows at Number 10 enjoying a pot of coffee and some biscuits while keeping an eye on Mossy in the cage trap to make sure he didn't escape. They had waited so long for something to be done about the foxes, they were too excited to sleep anyway, and they were both secretly thrilled that it had been in their garden that one was finally caught. Richard had gone outside briefly (wearing his wellington boots and a plastic hat) to poke through the bars of the cage with a stick, but Mossy had bared his teeth before grabbing hold of the stick and snapping it in two. 'A savage beast and no mistake,' concluded Mr Bingham before returning to the safety of his conservatory.

Zoe had just poured a second cup of coffee and asked Richard if he would like a chocolate finger when, to their astonishment, a large white goose waddled into view and began to honk loudly.

'Good heavens!' said Mrs Bingham. 'There's a goose on the patio!'

'Lord above, so there is,' exclaimed her husband.

Following Mr McNumpty's instructions, Snappy then waddled right up to the glass and began to peck the double glazing, all the while honking and quacking angrily.

'He's trying to break in! Shoo!' said Mrs Bingham, putting down her coffee cup. 'Do something, Richard!'

Richard banged on the glass from his side. 'Go away, you noisy bird!' he shouted, but this just seemed to make Snappy even more agitated. Snappy banged and pecked on the glass with increased speed and started to flap his wings to add to the sense of chaos.

While the Binghams were distracted, Miss Paulina was scurrying around the side of the house looking high and low for what Mr McNumpty had told her to find. 'Oh dear,' she muttered to herself. 'This does seem a rather naughty thing to be doing. But if it is for the greater good, then I must.' Finally she found what she was looking for: the telephone wire. With her sharp otter teeth she chomped through it in a single bite. Having completed her mission, she followed the next part of her instructions and gave a loud whistle.

At the back of Number 10, Mrs Bingham was getting quite upset. 'He's scratching the glass!' she said. 'Why is he doing this? Where did he come from? It's the middle of the night!'

Mr Bingham didn't know what to do about the angry goose that was attacking his property. He tried shouting, 'Boo! Boo! Go away!' He jumped up and down in his lounge, mimicking the goose and barking. But with no success.

Then suddenly, on hearing the whistle from Miss Paulina, Snappy stopped snapping. He did a big, wet goosey poo for good measure, then hurtled round the side of the house to the front door. So far everything was going according to plan. But his work wasn't done yet. Now he jumped onto the front doorstep and began to pound on the front door with his beak.

This was the signal for Craig, who had been hiding behind the hedge of Number 12. He no longer wore the pink slim-fit shirt or the inside-out trousers. He was on all fours and looked every inch the wild boar he really was. He strolled into the middle of the Binghams' front garden and began to dig up the flower bed with his trotters.

Alerted by the banging on the front door, Mr and Mrs Bingham had left their lounge and rushed fearfully to the bay window at the front of their property. Too scared to open their front door, they pulled back the fancy net curtains, peering round at their porch to see what on earth was happening now. But the first thing they saw was Craig, his muscular hairy grey back glistening in the rain, his big porky mouth full of marigolds, stomping on what was left of their summer flower display.

'W-w-what is THAT?' said Richard. 'Something wild and prehistoric!'

Zoe opened her mouth to scream in horror but no sound came out. Disappointed by the reaction and fearing that he maybe hadn't been noticed, Craig moved to the perfectly manicured lawn and began to gouge the velvety green surface with his tusks.

'Nooo!' pleaded Mr Bingham. 'Not my lawn too! What on earth is happening?'

'We're being invaded,' croaked Zoe. 'Call the police, Richard. Tell them we need an armed officer here right away! And hurry! I don't think I can take much more. My knees are beginning to buckle . . .'

Mr McNumpty had been watching the operation hidden between some parked cars on the other side of Fairfield Road with the remainder of his troops.

'Right,' he whispered urgently. 'So far so good. Bobby and Betty, you're next. Action!'

The twins darted across the deserted road and hid themselves in the shadows at the side of the Binghams' garage.

'Ready, sis?' asked Bobby breathlessly.

'Roger that!' said Betty. They both hunched down in preparation, counted: 'One, two, three!' in unison and leaped onto the garage roof. Then, tummies pressed to the tiles, they crept catlike to the far end and slid down into the cover of a hydrangea bush.

'There he is!' breathed Betty, pointing to the far end of the Binghams' back garden. 'By the compost heap!'

'I see him. Poor Mossy!' said Bobby. The fox, with nowhere to hide from the torrential rain, was sitting in a puddle, bedraggled and shivering. There looked to be very little fight left in him.

'Won't be long, Mossy!' said Betty in a loud whisper. 'We're coming to get you out of there.' Bobby went to run towards the fox, but Betty held him back.

'Wait,' she cautioned. 'We have to make sure the Binghams haven't come back to the lounge, remember?' The two young hyenas then poked their heads cautiously out of the bush and peered towards the back of the house.

'All clear,' said Betty, and they scampered across the garden towards the cage.

While all this was going on, inside the house Richard Bingham had discovered his phone wasn't working.

'The line's dead, Zoe,' he said in terror.

139

'I told you we should have got one of those mobile ones, Richard,' said his wife angrily. 'We've got to get out of here!' Outside they could hear the honking of a goose and the grunting of a wild boar. 'This is madness. You'll have to go out there and tackle that beast yourself.'

'But I can't go out THERE!' shuddered Mr Bingham.

'Be a man, Richard, for goodness' sake,' said Mrs Bingham. 'Think of the marigolds.'

Mr Bingham clenched his jaw. 'Very well, Zoe. If that's what you want. I will.' He glanced around the hallway for a suitable weapon.

From his hideout on the street, Mr McNumpty saw the front door of Number 10 slowly open.

A red tartan umbrella
(rolled up) poked out,
moving in circular
movements, followed
by Mr Bingham's
dressing-gown-clad arm.

'Gerroutahere!' he shouted
bravely as his slippered feet
stepped onto the doorstep.

Craig, who was by now enjoying a luxurious
mudbath in the flowerbed, raised his head
and snorted derisively.

'Go, Fred! Go, Amelia!' said Mr McNumpty.

At his command, Mr and Mrs Bold – unclothed
and in full hyena cry – charged menacingly
towards Mr Bingham, their teeth bared, jaws
drooling, piercing eyes fixed on their prey.

'Waaah!' screamed Mr Bingham and he swiftly retreated back inside his front door. There was the sound of bolts being drawn and keys being turned.

By this time the twins had got to the cage and after a moment or two had worked out how to unlock the door.

'Come on, Mossy,' they urged the hunched, broken fox. 'Quickly. Come with us. You're free.'

Mossy was
shivering now
and too cold and
tired to speak, but
slowly, cautiously,
he got to his feet.

Mr and Mrs Bold, their work done at the front of Number 10, were now at the twins' side, and with their encouragement Mossy was quickly ushered through the other gardens of Fairfield Road, to the back door and into the safety of the kitchen at Number 41.

Mr McNumpty then gave the signal to Miss Paulina who whistled the 'withdraw' command to Craig and Snappy, and Fairfield Road was quiet and empty once again.

Chapter 12

By now it was almost dawn, and there was a lot of cleaning up to do. The kitchen floor at Number 41 was covered in mud and all of those involved in the rescue of Mossy were wet and cold and in need of a good clean-up. But no one seemed to care. Releasing their natural animal behaviour had been entirely enjoyable for everyone, and the steamy, muddy troop decided that for this night only, they should just go with the flow and revel in the dirty, smelly joy of it all. Besides, getting clean and presentable wasn't their immediate priority. Mossy was.

He was sat in front of the electric fire and given a bowl of water and some lamb chops. He stared into the distance while Sylvie sat by his side but he didn't say much.

'Well done, everyone,' said Mr McNumpty, rubbing his head dry with a towel. 'Top work! And in such terrible weather too!'

What happens when it rains cats and dogs?

You have to be careful not to step in a poodle!

Mrs Bold glared at her husband.

'Mossy?' she asked. 'Are you OK now?'

'I'm very cross with myself,' said Mossy after a pause.

'You mustn't be,' said Mrs Bold. 'Those traps are terrible things.'

'Yes, but I knew that,' said Mossy angrily. 'How could I have been so stupid? It was the cheese. I was hungry and the smell of it just tempted me. It was Moose cheese . . . A rare delicacy. How could I resist? In my eagerness to taste it I was careless. I've stolen the bait out of those cage traps countless times before and always got away with it.'

'Well not to worry. It's a good job we came along when we did.'

'Oh, I'd have got out of there, don't you worry,' said Mossy, not sounding in the least bit grateful.

'Mossy,' said Sylvie. 'That's not true. You were completely trapped in there and if it

147

hadn't been for these wonderful animals—'

'Oh, shut your mouth, vixen,' he snapped. 'They're not animals. They're would-be humans and I owe them nothing.'

Everyone was shocked.

'Now if you don't mind, I'd like to go to sleep. I presume there's a room for me upstairs? Perhaps I can bunk in with the goose,' he offered, licking his snout.

'No, no,' said Snappy, suddenly not as snappy as usual. 'By all means have my room,' he offered. 'I'll share with Craig.'

'Much obliged,' said Mossy. 'Well goodnight,

all. Sylvie, say goodnight.'

And they went upstairs, leaving the rescuers open-mouthed below.

The next day at 41 Fairfield Road there was an almighty clean-up operation. All the residents and guests had to be showered, dried and brushed, after which the kitchen, bathroom and more or less the whole house had to be scrubbed, mopped and hoovered. There were several buckets full of mud and fur and a few flower petals. Mrs Bold had an idea that these could all be recycled into some lovely hats, so they were kept outside the back door ready for when she was in a creative mood.

Fun as it had been to be 'wild' again for a few hours, it was not to be repeated. The antics of the night before had been necessary to rescue Mossy but tails must be hidden again, clothes must be worn and everyone had to be reminded to walk and talk like humans. And no one could suppose that Mr and Mrs Bingham would let the matter lie. There was (what was left of) the flowerbed in their front garden for a start. Evidence of the terror they had been subjected to was there for all to see.

Uncle Tony went for a casual stroll past Number 10 mid-morning, with Miranda in her pushchair, and sure enough, a police car was parked outside and a reporter and a photographer were in the front garden taking pictures of Craig's muddy trotter prints. The journalist asked Uncle Tony if he lived locally and if he'd heard 'anything unusual' the night before.

'Like what?' asked Tony.

'Er, a goose? A wild boar? Couple of wild dogs with frothing mouths, a bit like hyenas?' asked the reporter hopefully.

'No. But I did see a herd of elephants. And a flying saucer,' replied Tony. 'Never heard such nonsense!' And then he walked away chuckling to himself.

It was generally thought amongst the residents of Fairfield Road that the Binghams had been the victims of youthful high jinks. Some over-refreshed chaps from Kingston University had maybe dressed up in costumes as a prank. Or, it was whispered, maybe too much cheese at bedtime?

Chapter

So you might think this story is almost finished: Mossy had learned his lesson and would steal from the houses of Fairfield Road no more, and life could return to normal.

But you'd be wrong. You can generally work out when you're coming to the end of a book because there aren't many pages left. As you can tell, we're far from done with this tale. Barely halfway through, in fact. There's going to be what is known in literary circles as a plot development. Stand by.

Mr and Mrs Bold thought it wise for Mossy

and Sylvie to lay low at Number 41 for a few days while everything calmed down.

'Too much fuss in Fairfield Road!' said Mr Bold.

Mossy grudgingly agreed. Sylvie seemed pleased to have other animals to talk to, although as the days went by she began to miss living in the park. She was a shy fox, but she got on very well with Mrs Bold and they often had a nice chat together while Mossy was having an afternoon nap. Bit by bit she began to tell Mrs Bold about her life in the park – and how she had ended up with the bad-tempered Mossy.

'He wasn't always like he is now,' she said apologetically. 'But he's angry, you see. You'll understand *why* when I explain. Mossy had – well, still has – a brother. Bert. They were always very close. Inseparable. Two handsome, intelligent foxes. Strong and fit. Much admired and respected by all the other foxes. They would hunt together in the park, flirt with us vixens – me in particular. In fact Bert was my first true love. I always believed we'd end up together. But Bert was ambitious. He wanted more out of life. Like yourselves. Bert thought his best chance of doing that was as a human. He tried to persuade me and Mossy that we could live a different life but we didn't feel like him and I don't think we believed he would ever do it.

'Then one day he did. He left. Mossy and I were broken-hearted. Mossy took it badly. He was grief-stricken and very angry.'

'So that's why he's so rude about our way of life!' exclaimed Mrs Bold.

'Exactly.' Sylvie nodded sadly. 'Mossy and I became closer in our grief. And when I realised Bert wouldn't be coming back, I agreed to be Mossy's vixen. But he's different from Bert. Maybe it's because he's so angry. I feel disloyal saying this but he's cruel at times, unkind and cold. And particularly when it comes to humans and their way of life.'

'Oh, I see.'

'Mossy won't let me out of his sight. He's afraid that I'll follow Bert one day. But I'll never do that. No offence, but I don't want to be a human.'

'If you don't mind me asking, why do you stay with Mossy?' said Mrs Bold. 'He does seem rather unkind.'

'I've asked myself that many a time, Mrs

Bold, and when I see how happy you are with Mr Bold I do wish things could be different. But deep down I know Mossy is just upset, that he can change, and that if I leave him too he'll feel even worse.'

Mrs Bold gave the vixen a sad smile. 'So you never saw Bert again?'

'Just once. He came back about a year later. He was dressed in overalls, said he had a job nearby. That life was good. He begged Mossy and I to join him. But Mossy wouldn't talk about it. Accused Bert of betrayal.'

'And is that when the stealing started?' asked Mrs Bold.

'Correct,' said Sylvie. 'It seems to give Mossy great pleasure to invade human homes and steal food and belongings. As if this is revenge on Bert, in some way.'

Mrs Bold gave Sylvie a comforting rub on her shoulder.

'Poor Mossy. And poor Sylvie. It can't be much fun living with someone who is so miserable all the time.'

Sylvie shook her head. 'Well, no it isn't. But I remember the old Mossy,' she said. 'He's missing his brother, that's all. Maybe one day he can be happy again. Maybe we both can. I really hope so. But it's not the same without Bert. He had a loud, joyful laugh. I can't bear to think I'll never hear that sound again.' Sylvie stared into the distance, lost in her memories.

'Ah, yes,' smiled Mrs Bold. 'Laughter is so important in life. As a hyena I'd have to say that it is the most important thing.'

Chapter

'I'm going to make a **hat** today!' announced Mrs Bold the next morning, placing the buckets of dried mud and fur on the draining board. 'The twins have gone round to Minnie's house so do you fancy giving me a hand, Sylvie?'

Sylvie looked a little nervous, Mossy was asleep upstairs. In fact since he arrived, he spent most of his time eating, sleeping or teasing poor Snappy.

'**Come on**, Sylvie,' urged Mrs Bold. 'It'll be fun. Take your mind off missing the park so much.'

'Oh, well, I'm not sure I'll be any good. What sort of hat?'

'A very unusual one! Now, my dear, could you run some water from the tap into that bucket full of mud? Not too much – just enough to turn it into clay again.'

Sylvie – a wild fox with no training about how to act like a human – jumped up onto the kitchen counter and turned on the tap with her teeth.

Mrs Bold took a wooden spoon and stirred the earth with the water until it was a lovely grey gooey mess.

'Perfect!' she announced. 'Now you see that round mixing bowl? Could you pop it on your head for me please? Upside down?'

'Er, like this?' asked Sylvie, unsure. Her head was completely inside the bowl.

'Excellent! Hold still!' Mrs Bold then got a soup ladle from the kitchen drawer and poured some mud gently over the upside-down bowl and patted it into place with her paws.

'Coming along nicely,' she told Sylvie, and then got some of the fur, feathers and squashed flowers she'd collected from Craig and Snappy and arranged them tastefully on the top. The whole creation was then gently removed from Sylvie's head and placed on a baking tray to set.

'One hat completed!' said Amelia looking admiringly at her handiwork. 'And there's enough mud here for at least two more! These will go down very well with my customers at the market.'

Half an hour later there were three mud bonnets sitting proudly in a row. Balanced on the draining board still, Sylvie cocked her head to one side. 'Pretty. But what if it rains? Won't the mud melt?'

'Um.' Mrs Bold clearly hadn't thought of this. 'So glad you think they're pretty . . .' she said brightly.

Just then they heard Mossy calling for Sylvie from the spare bedroom upstairs.

'I'd better go,' said Sylvie, a rather worried tone to her voice. 'He's woken up. Might be hungry again.'

'Can't he make his own snack?' asked Mrs Bold innocently.

But Sylvie had jumped down onto the kitchen floor and hurried upstairs. She was back in thirty seconds. 'He wants sausage and mash and three chocolate éclairs,' she said. 'And he wants it now!'

Very demanding! thought Mrs Bold to herself. *But at least he's safe here, and not stealing food from anywhere.*

Mossy was certainly a hungry fox. When Mr

Bold was trying to persuade him to stay in the safety of Number 41 for a while, and not risk encountering the pest control people outside, Mossy had asked what sort of food would be provided.

'We'll feed you anything you want!' said Mr Bold.

'Anything?' repeated Mossy suspiciously.

'Yes,' pleaded Fred. 'Your lives are at stake!'

'Right. Then talking of steak, that is what I'd like. Three of them for my tea. Sirloin. Large. Organic. And then rhubarb and custard for pudding.'

'Oh, er, no problem,' said Mr Bold. 'I'll pop to the supermarket right away. But before I go . . .'

165

Did you hear about the man who went to the doctor with rhubarb sticking out of each ear and custard up his nose?

The doctor told him to eat more sensibly!

By the time Mossy had been living with the Bolds for a week, his scratches had healed and he was completely recovered. In fact he'd eaten well and done no exercise whatsoever, so he was looking very contented indeed. With no more reports of any fox thefts or invasions, the residents of Fairfield Road presumed they'd seen the last of them and life had returned to normal. The pest control vans were no longer cruising the streets of Teddington and the sense of fear and suspicion was gone.

'I think,' whispered Mrs Bold to her husband, when they were tucked up in bed that evening, 'it might be safe for Mossy and Sylvie to return to Bushy Park. No one seems to believe the Binghams' story of wild hyenas in the street so hopefully everything has died down. I'll miss Sylvie, though. She's such a gentle, helpful fox and so good with the children.'

'Yes, Bobby and Betty seem very fond of her too.'

'I'm sure she'll make a wonderful mother herself one day, but I really think Mossy would be an awful father. He's so bullying and rude and greedy.'

'Yes I know. And do you know what his favourite food is?' asked Mr Bold.

'Seconds!' chortled Amelia.

The two hyenas had to put their heads under the pillow in case their foxy visitors overheard them laughing.

'But you're right,' said Fred once he was able to speak again. 'So long as Mossy doesn't get up to his old tricks again, they should be fine and it's time they left. We can't afford to keep feeding them, and Mossy is so rude about our way of life, I'm sure he'll be pleased to go. We can drop off the odd food parcel for them to make sure he doesn't go back to his old stealing ways, but I'm sure he's learned his lesson. He is bound to be glad to get back to the park and his life as a wild animal. We'll tell them tomorrow at breakfast. After he's eaten. He's always in a better mood then.'

Chapter

Breakfast at the Bolds' was always a busy, jolly affair. There were three sittings, because not everyone could fit round the table at once. The twins and Mr and Mrs Bold were first, and they had cereal and toast with peanut butter. Mr Bold always had some jokes to try out that he'd thought of in the shower.

> Did you hear about the man who slept under a tractor?

> He wanted to wake up oily in the morning!

Laughing with their mouths full and **spluttering** bits of cornflake and crumbs over the table was, I'm afraid, an **inevitable** side effect of such hilarity.

When the Bolds had finished, it was the turn of Uncle Tony, Miranda and the students. Tony liked porridge with honey, Miranda enjoyed a fruit salad, and Craig the wild boar had mushrooms on toast. Miss Paulina the otter had kippers, and Snappy the goose pecked at some muesli and prunes and enjoyed spitting the stones at Miss Paulina, who endured the nuisance with a saintly expression on her face. Mr Bold usually did the washing-up, but had plenty more jokes to start everyone's day off with a laugh.

What did the cat say when he lost his money?

'I'm paw!'

What do you get if you cross a llama with a tortoise?

A turtleneck sweater!

What game should you never, ever play with unicorns?

Leapfrog!

The final sitting was for Mossy and Sylvie. Mossy didn't like to get up early, and his 'order' was usually quite challenging. And that morning was no different.

'I want a fry-up today,' he barked – there was never a please or thank you from Mossy. 'That means jumbo sausages, three rashers of streaky bacon, two fried eggs – duck or quail, I can't abide hen's eggs – grilled tomato, button mushrooms, black pudding, baked beans and crispy hash browns. Then I'll be ready for a toasted muffin, smoked salmon with hollandaise sauce, sprinkled with chopped chives. And don't be mean with the salmon. Then I'll finish with some crunchy granola layered with fresh strawberries and raspberries, natural full-fat yoghurt and blueberry compote. And give me a freshly ground espresso while I'm waiting.' Mr Bold rolled his eyes at Mrs Bold and started cooking.

'What about you, Sylvie?'

'Just a cup of tea please, Amelia,' said the vixen, looking embarrassed. 'And a slice of dry toast if you can spare it.'

With such a lot of food to get through, you'd think Mossy's breakfast would take hours, but once it was ready he wolfed it down hungrily and then gave a satisfied burp. Mrs Bold nudged Fred and mouthed the words: 'Do it now!'

'Ahem,' began Mr Bold. 'Breakfast to your liking?' he began.

'It was OK,' said Mossy. 'The tomato was a little soft. And I'll have extra sausages tomorrow.'

'Ah. Righto,' said Fred. 'Only we were thinking. Once it gets dark tonight we reckon it would be perfectly safe for you and Sylvie to go home to Bushy Park. Lovely for you, eh? Get back to your old foxy ways? Bet you've missed that. Although, of course, no more invading the bins and stealing food from houses. Lesson learned, wouldn't you say?'

There was an awkward silence. Mossy stared at his empty plate and Sylvie watched him wide-eyed with trepidation.

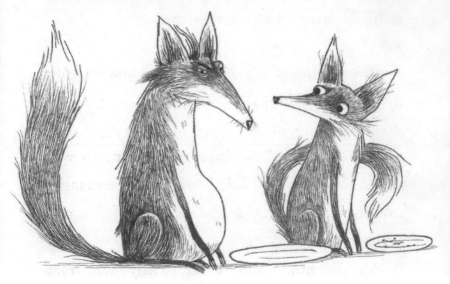

'I expect,' continued Mrs Bold breezily, 'you must be missing your old den. Shouldn't leave it for too long. Badgers might move in. It's been lovely having you here but—'

'GO HOME?' boomed Mossy. 'You must be joking! It's not safe out there with all those dangerous humans. And I hate humans. Sylvie and I are staying put.'

Mr and Mrs Bold's eyes widened and they stared at Mossy, then at each other. It was really a rather awkward situation.

'But having you here was only a temporary arrangement,' said Mr Bold reasonably. 'We don't really have the space or money to house more animals. It can't go on for ever.'

'Yes it can. And it will,' said Mossy decisively. 'We're *far* better off here. It's safe. We're well fed – well, most of the time. This is five-star accommodation. Maybe four and a half, given the mushy tomato. I've had to mark you down for that. Why would we want to go back to living in the park and scavenging

176

for our dinner? We're staying here.'

Mr and Mrs Bold did the only thing they (as hyenas) could do in the circumstances: they laughed. A forced laugh to begin with, but as the reality of the situation became apparent, together with the knowledge that they were stuck with unwanted guests for the foreseeable future, a kind of desperate, hysterical laughter took hold until they were literally crying.

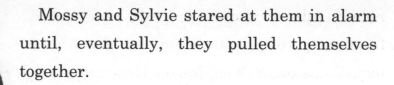

Mossy and Sylvie stared at them in alarm until, eventually, they pulled themselves together.

'Oh dear, do forgive us,' said Mrs Bold, wiping her eyes. 'It's just that, for a moment we thought you meant you would be staying with us for ever!'

'That's right, yes,' said Mossy.

'You mean you'd like to become Bold students? Learn to live like humans and then, er, move on to an exciting new life?' asked Mr Bold hopefully.

'Yuck. No. I've told you. I hate humans. I'm a fox and I like being a fox,' growled Mossy. 'I'm a fox for ever and this is my for ever home. And that reminds me. I hate sleeping on a bed. I want a fox den in our room. Order a tonne of earth, would you, from the garden centre? Now I'm going for a nap. Come on, Sylvie.' Mossy then sauntered out of the kitchen. Sylvie, head bowed, followed behind him. But before Mr or Mrs Bold could say anything, he returned.

'And don't think about trying to get us out. We know all your secrets, remember? I'd hate to be the one who puts an end to your domestic bliss.' He chuckled to himself. 'Pest control would have a field day round here, wouldn't they, if your secret got out? Walking, talking hyenas and a grizzly bear! A monkey and a wild boar! You'd be on the front page of every newspaper.'

'Now listen, Mossy,' began Mr Bold. 'You can't be serious?'

'Shut it!' snapped Mossy. 'I'm serious, all

right? So unless you fancy seeing your family split up and carted off to the zoo – that's if they don't shoot the lot of you – I suggest you do as I say. You've been outfoxed, mate. Who's laughing now, eh? Ha!' Mossy gave an evil laugh of his own, then cocked his leg on the kitchen door and left, his long, bushy red tail swaying from side to side as he walked regally down the hall towards the stairs.

As soon as they were alone, Mrs Bold flung her arms round Mr Bold, clinging to him. 'Oh, Fred! What are we going to do?' she wailed. 'We can't let him treat us like this!'

Mr Bold patted his wife's back. 'There now, Amelia,' he comforted her. 'It'll be all right. I'll think of something.'

'But we can't let him blackmail us like this. It's . . . criminal!'

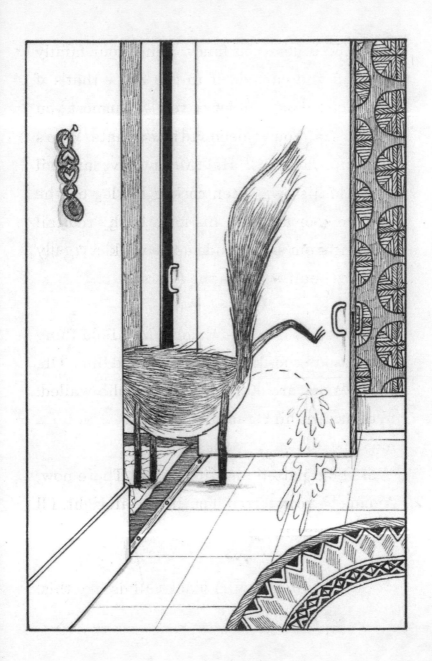

'I know. There **must** be something we can do. I need to have a think.' Fred sat Amelia on a chair and got her a glass of water.

'And **meanwhile**?'

'Well, er . . .' He shrugged.

'Just don't make a joke, dear,' pleaded Mrs Bold. 'I don't think there is **anything** that could make me laugh right now.' Fred thought for a moment. But he was stumped.

'No,' he answered. 'For once, I don't think there is either.'

Chapter

There are times when grown-ups think it best not to tell children the truth. But the children usually guess anyway.

Like if Twitchy the hamster sadly dies and the adults don't want the children to be upset, they replace it with another one that looks about the same and hope the children don't notice. Except the new Twitchy has a brown patch on his leg that wasn't there before – not to mention longer whiskers and a rather grumpy personality. So the children soon guess. They're not stupid. And sometimes the children don't want to upset their parents by telling them they've guessed there is a new Twitchy in the old Twitchy's place, and the whole thing gets rather complicated. Everyone is so busy pretending, trying not to upset everyone else, it can get rather, well, upsetting.

So while Mr and Mrs Bold tried to smile and carry on as normal in front of the twins, Betty and Bobby soon noticed something wasn't quite right. For a start, their parents had stopped laughing. Mrs Bold frowned, despite herself, whenever Mossy was around, and a worried look would cross their father's face as he wrote down Mossy's latest food order. Caviar and foie gras were very expensive snacks, everyone knew that. How could their parents afford them? And why did they never say no to Mossy?

Then there was the skip full of soil that appeared on the drive one day when the twins came home from school with Minnie.

'Is that for your garden?' asked Minnie.

'No, afraid not,' said Mr Bold, wiping the sweat from his brow as he shovelled it into a wheelbarrow. 'Mossy wants it to build a den in his room upstairs.'

The wheelbarrow was trundled through the house to the foot of the stairs and then Mr Bold and Mr McNumpty transported it upstairs by the bucketload while Mrs Bold looked very worried about her carpet.

Mr Bold half-heartedly made some jokes.

What did the big bucket say to the little bucket?

You look a little pail!

What's worse than raining buckets?

Hailing taxis!

The twins laughed, but Mr McNumpty was panting for breath and didn't join in.

Moving the earth upstairs took several days.

'Why are they doing this?' Bobby asked his sister. 'If I asked to build a den in my bedroom with all that muck they'd say no for sure.'

'Well I've noticed that Mum and Dad do whatever Mossy asks,' shrugged Betty.

'Me too,' said Bobby. 'I don't like the way he speaks to them. Or Sylvie. *Or us!*'

'He's rude and horrid,' agreed Betty. 'And I wish he'd move out. I know we always welcome animals to our house. And I know we're always helpful. But most animals are friendly and grateful. Sometimes I wish we'd just left him in that stupid cage.'

'And he isn't making any effort to live like a human, so what's the point of him being here?' asked Bobby. '*And* he eats SO much food! Mum has to go shopping twice a day.'

Betty nodded thoughtfully.

'There is something going on,' she told her brother. 'But I've no idea what it is . . .'

Then the next Saturday something odd happened. When the twins came downstairs for breakfast, Mr Bold wasn't there.

'Where's Dad?' asked Bobby.

'Gone to work,' said Mrs Bold, pouring cereal into a bowl.

'But it's Saturday!' pointed out Betty, outraged. 'We always wash the Honda together, then go to the sweet shop!'

'Well not today, I'm afraid,' said their mother, trying unsuccessfully to sound bright and breezy. 'Overtime. A rush on for more jokes at the Christmas cracker factory, so that'll be useful to pay all the food bills.' Mrs Bold then glanced up at the ceiling, as if the 'useful' part referred to Mossy.

I'm afraid the truth was that the food bills were now so big that Mr Bold had had no option but to take on extra work at the factory, otherwise the rest of the family would have had to start going hungry.

Bobby looked despondent. He'd been looking forward to washing the car as usual with his sister and father, and then choosing some chocolate at the shop.

'Never mind,' said Mrs Bold. 'You can come to the market with *me* for a change, and help me sell my novelty hats.'

Teddington market was held every Saturday afternoon in Church Street. It was popular and lively and rather up-market: there were stalls for ceramics, posh pasties, organic pet food, vintage vinyl, flowers, tasty hot food and glittery mobile phone accessories. Mrs Bold's fancy hats stall was very popular and because her home-made hats were so unusual, people came back every week to see what her latest creations were.

Mrs Bold, you may have heard, can make hats out of anything you might imagine: pegs, broken plates, empty baked bean tins, old clocks, dead mice: you think of it and Mrs

Bold will make a hat out of it. Smart ladies of Teddington ſnaₚ up the hats each week and wear them to church on Sunday morning or to weddings or on holiday. The ladies compete with each other to see who is wearing the 'lₐteſt' design, and in fashionable circles Mrs Bold's wit and originality are much praised.

Mrs Bold was very pleased with her latest hats, which were the mud and feather bonnets she had made with Sylvie's help following the night of Mossy's rescue. Not as tall or spectacular as some of her previous offerings, but surprisingly chIc and retro in a rustic sort of way.

The twins helped their mother set up the stall and put all the hats on display.

Mrs Bold bought the twins a hot dog each, but was then rather busy with her customers. When their best friend Minnie wandered into the market, looking for a little coat for her dog Walter, Bobby and Betty were delighted.

'Hi, Betty! Hi, Bobby! Didn't expect to see you here,' she said. 'Don't you usually wash the car with your dad on Saturdays?'

'Dad had to go to work,' said Bobby sadly. 'His boss needs more jokes apparently. So we had to come and help Mum sell her hats.'

'Throwing wet sponges around is definitely more fun than selling hats,' concluded Betty. 'We're so bored.'

Minnie thought for a moment. 'Why don't we help your dad?' she asked.

'How?' said Betty.

'Well, we could make up some jokes for him. And there are lots of people here at the market. Why don't we ask everyone we see if they know any funny jokes?'

'Brill idea!' said Bobby. 'Then when Dad comes home we can tell him all the jokes we've collected!'

'And he won't need to do overtime again!' added Betty, jumping up and down with excitement.

Mrs Bold also thought Minnie's idea was an excellent one – and it would keep the twins occupied too. There was some empty space at the end of her stall, now that several hats had already been sold, so Betty, Bobby and Minnie set up their JOKES WANTED! shop, quickly making a sign with a marker pen on an old cardboard box.

'Roll up! Roll up!' called Bobby. 'Jokes wanted here please! Old jokes, new jokes – we'll take them all. No joke considered too old or corny. We're not fussy!'

Betty and Minnie stood by hopefully with a pencil and notepad.

'What do we get for 'em?' asked a bald man with tattoos, who'd wandered over from the nearby fruit and veg stall.

'Er, we'll take them off your hands for you,' said Betty. 'No charge!'

'They'll go to a very good home,' promised Minnie. 'And make people happy.'

The bald man rubbed his chin. 'OK,' he said.

What do you get if you cross a sheepdog with a rose?

A collie-flower!

Several of Mrs Bold's customers had overheard the joke and chuckled to themselves.

'Actually,' said a woman in a floral dress, who had just purchased a turban-style hat made out of a coiled-up draught excluder with a candle stuck in the top, 'I've got an old joke I'd like to get shot of.' She cleared her throat.

How do you make a tissue dance?

Put a little boogey in it!

There was a roar of laughter from the bald man.

What do you call a baby monkey?

A chimp off the old block!

Soon the jokes stall had attracted a crowd and the jokes were coming thick and fast.

Why was the belt arrested?

Because he held up some trousers!

Everyone was so busy telling jokes and laughing at them, no one noticed the smart, shiny Rolls Royce that purred silently to a halt a few metres away. The tinted rear window opened a few centimetres and an elegant gloved hand emerged and pointed at one of Mrs Bold's hats. The chauffeur then got out of the driver's seat, slipped through the crowd, purchased two mud bonnets from Mrs Bold and drove away.

Chapter

When Mr Bold returned from work later that evening looking tired and drawn, he was thrilled with the jokes the twins and Minnie had collected for him.

'Thank you so much,' he said, shaking his head in wonderment. 'These are great. And worth quite a lot! What wonderful pups you are.'

Minnie giggled.

The twins and Minnie – who was staying for tea – felt very proud of themselves. They'd had a fun day and helped Mr Bold at the same time. Both Mr and Mrs Bold looked much happier that evening.

'We'll do the jokes stall again next week, if Mum says it's OK,' said Bobby.

'Yes of course, dear,' said Mrs Bold, who was making a spaghetti bolognese. 'I'm all for it. And it attracted lots of new customers for my hats. I sold all three mud bonnets today and made more money than usual, which will come in very useful,' she said, glancing at her husband. 'And it's given me an idea to make some new hats out of unusual material. How about muesli glued together with chocolate sauce? Edible hats could become all the rage.'

Mr Bold said, 'Lovely. And think of all the seagulls and pigeons that will attract. Swooping down to peck at the ladies' heads!'

The thought of this made everyone laugh so much they had to have some lemonade to calm themselves down.

After tea the twins and Minnie went out to play in the garden while Mr and Mrs Bold cleared the table and then laid it again for Uncle Tony, Miranda and the students. Mr Bold tried out the new jokes and everyone laughed appreciatively. Then there was more washing-up to do until finally two bowls of spaghetti bolognese were placed on the floor for Mossy and Sylvie. Mossy wouldn't dream of eating from a table and wouldn't allow Sylvie to either. 'We're foxes, remember?'

It was hard to forget it, these days. A pungent, foxy aroma emanated from the earth den in the bedroom and filled the whole house. You could barely open the door for the mound of earth. There was a small round entrance

'Thank you. But grateful as I am for your hospitality, I'm really missing the park,' said Sylvie. 'The fresh air and the other foxes. Mossy must be too, underneath all the bluff and bluster. He doesn't really want to live in a human house. I will keep trying to persuade him and I'm sure he'll decide we ought to go back soon.'

'I hope so,' said Mrs Bold. 'You have a right to be happy. We all do.'

Mr Bold had by now found a local garage that was willing to help with the broken-down Honda, and a man in overalls was looking inside the bonnet. After a few minutes and a lot of tapping and some sort of wrenching with a spanner, the mechanic wiped his hands with an oily rag and gave his verdict.

'Well, mate. It's your pistons. Welded against your cylinder walls, I'm afraid.'

'Oh,' said Mr Bold. 'Naughty pistons, eh? Will it take long to fix? Only I've got a hungry fox – I mean hungry fella at home waiting for his dinner, you see.'

He was half a mile from home when disaster struck. The Honda began to cough and splutter.

'Oh dear,' he said to the car. 'Please don't break down now, little car. I dread to think what Mossy will do if he doesn't get his dinner!'

But it was no good – after a final shudder, the Honda's engine cut out and Mr Bold just had time to steer it into a side street before it stopped altogether.

Back at Fairfield Road, Sylvie and Mrs Bold were discussing the future.

'I do feel bad about overstaying our welcome,' said Sylvie. 'Mossy is being very unreasonable. I've tried to speak to him about it but he just won't listen.'

'It's not your fault,' said Amelia. 'I know that. Everyone is welcome in our house for as long as they want to stay. It's just the cost of all the food Mossy requires and the way he treats us that is so unacceptable.'

'I heard what he said to you,' said Sylvie, pacing up and down and looking concerned. 'He's blackmailing you, isn't he? Threatening to tell people who you really are. I'm so sorry.'

Mrs Bold nodded and a tear rolled down her cheek. 'Mr Bold says it will work itself out one day. We just have to be patient. He is not the sort to let anything get him down for long. Maybe he's right. Certainly the twins' joke stall today was a great help bringing in extra money to pay for all the, er, extras. So we'll cope, I guess. And you, Sylvie, are more than welcome here. I like having you around. And I couldn't have made those mud bonnets without you.'

'I'll look after Amelia,' said Sylvie, emerging from under the table. 'You go. Hurry.'

As soon as Mr Bold had gone, Sylvie and Amelia cleaned up the spaghetti bolognese with some kitchen towel.

'Sorry about the mess and the waste,' said Sylvie.

'It's not your fault, dear,' said Mrs Bold. But she knew the situation couldn't continue like this for much longer. Mossy was ruling the roost, and there had to be a way to fight back. They just hadn't thought of it yet.

Chapter

Mr Bold whizzed around the supermarket, grabbing two juicy steaks, carrots, chips, cheesecake and a top-of-the-range box of chocolates, and was back in the Honda in record time. He amused himself while driving home by telling himself jokes.

Mossy, his eyes flashing with anger as he moved towards Mrs Bold. Mr Bold jumped in front of his wife protectively.

'Now then, Mossy. No need to overreact. I'm just going to the supermarket, as it happens. What can I get you? A nice big steak?'

Mossy sat down and licked his paw.

'That's more like it,' he said calmly. Then he gave a big yellow-fanged yawn. 'I'll have two T-bone steaks. Triple-fried crinkle-cut chips with sautéed carrots. Then a vanilla cheesecake. And a box of chocolates to finish.'

'Of course!' said Mr Bold. 'Now why don't you go upstairs for a little nap in your cosy den and I'll call when it's ready for you?'

Mr Bold's obsequious manner seemed to please Mossy and a slight smile hovered on his lips. 'Clean this mess up, vixen,' he said to Sylvie, then sashayed out of the kitchen and back upstairs.

Being aware that any unnecessary delay might anger the hungry fox, Mr Bold gave his worried-looking wife a hug and grabbed the car keys. 'I'll be as quick as I can,' he said. 'Stay out of his way.'

concealed behind a rose bush that Mossy had demanded be uprooted from the front garden. And because Mossy was eating so much and getting hardly any exercise, this entrance had been widened several times in the last few days.

'What's this?' asked Mossy, sniffing at his dinner suspiciously that evening. Mr and Mrs Bold could tell from the weary expression on Sylvie's face that Mossy was in a particularly bad mood.

'It's spaghetti bolognese,' said Mr Bold.

'Delicious!' added Mrs Bold hopefully.

Mossy took another sniff and wrinkled his nose. 'Well I'm not eating it,' he said. 'Smells disgusting. Foreign muck. Make me something else.'

'That's all there is,' said Mrs Bold. Mossy glared at her.

In an attempt to lighten the atmosphere, Mr Bold asked:

Did you hear about the Italian chef who was very ill?

He pasta way!

But not even Mrs Bold laughed at the joke.

Mossy's response was to swipe the bowl angrily with his paw, overturning it and spilling his unwanted dinner across the floor. Mrs Bold jumped and Sylvie darted under the table for cover.

'ALL THERE IS, did you say?' growled

'I'll have to tow it back to the garage, I'm afraid,' said the mechanic. 'Should be ready later this week though. I'll drop you home, if it's not *too* far. Where do you live?'

'How kind of you,' said Mr Bold. 'I'll tell you some jokes on the way! I live at 41 Fairfield Road. Just by Bushy Park. Do you know it?'

'Oh yes,' answered the mechanic somewhat wistfully. 'I know the park very well.'

Mr Bold was true to his word and the whole way back home he told endless jokes, which the mechanic thought were very funny. Jokes like:

What made the dinosaur's car stop?

A flat Tyre-annosaurus!

'We're here now,' said the mechanic. 'I'll drop the car off in the week.'

'Thank you so much,' said Mr Bold, shaking his hand and getting out of the car with his shopping. 'My name is Fred Bold.'

'Thanks for the jokes, mate. Brightened my day up no end, you have!' said the mechanic. 'My name is Bert.'

And Mr Bold went indoors and cooked Mossy his two steaks, chips and sautéed carrots.

Chapter

But that night Mr Bold tossed and turned in his bed. Unable to sleep, he went downstairs for a glass of water. Mrs Bold, realising her husband wasn't next to her, came downstairs too and found him staring out of the kitchen window.

'Couldn't you sleep, dear?' she said, putting her paw on his back.

'Oh, Amelia, this just can't go on,' said Mr Bold. 'Even my children are working on Saturdays to feed this greedy animal. He's threatened *you*, he's cruel to Sylvie and he's blackmailing us and threatening all our safety and happiness. He's a bully. And we're allowing him to bully us. I would never have let this happen in Africa. I would have stood up to a predator. But I'm so desperate to protect our way of life, I'm letting him beat me.'

'I agree. But what else can we do?' said Amelia. 'You're doing this to protect us. I'm quite sure if you fought it out with him you could win, my darling. But a fox and hyena fighting would alert the neighbours and our secret would definitely be discovered. And if we throw Mossy out and demand he leaves then I'm pretty sure he'll reveal our secret without a moment's hesitation. I think all we can do is carry on as we are and hope that eventually he misses his wild ways so much he decides to move on.'

'We've thought that for too long,' said Mr Bold. 'We're putting up with his behaviour, hoping something will change. It's what Sylvie's done for a long time but it hasn't worked for her and it isn't working for us. We're frightened of what he will do and we are living in fear in our own home. Well no more.'

'What are you going to do?' asked Mrs Bold. 'Please be careful. I'd rather live like this than have my family imprisoned in a zoo or a cage.'

'But don't you see? We're already imprisoned – in our own home. And it's time we broke free.'

'How can we stop a bully being a bully?'

Mr Bold scratched his head for a moment.

'Well you can't. But you can make it difficult for them. After all, there's only one of him. Together with us Bolds, there is Minnie, Walter, the students, Uncle Tony, Mr McNumpty and Miranda. That's twelve!'

'And Sylvie makes thirteen!' corrected Mrs Bold.

'Strength in numbers! That's the answer!' exclaimed Fred, beaming at his wife. 'Right. I need a pen and paper. And some cardboard and felt-tip pens . . . I'm going to be busy . . . Tomorrow things are going to be different!'

The next morning when the twins came down to the kitchen for breakfast there was a surprise waiting for them. Hanging from all the kitchen cupboards, on the walls and even from the ceiling were brightly coloured posters. Mr and Mrs Bold stood huddled by the back door looking pleased with themselves, gently quivering with amusement.

It took the twins a few minutes to read the MANY posters and notices their parents had made.

'Bully-Free Zone!' said the biggest sign, above the kitchen window. As they scanned the room they read them all out loud.

Dont have a Fight - have a Laugh!
Smile at Bullies They HATE it
ALL BULLIES ARE COWARDS
TRY Saying Something NICE
WHY ARE BULLIES Like Skeletons? They don't have GUTS!

'Wow,' said Bobby. 'This is amazing!'

'We've been rather busy,' said Mr Bold proudly. 'But hopefully it will give Mossy something to think about when he comes down for breakfast.'

'Er,' interrupted Betty. 'There's only one problem.'

'What's that?' asked Mrs Bold.

'Mossy can't read,' said Betty.

There was an awkward silence.

'He can't?' said Mr Bold.

'No, Dad,' said Betty, shaking her head sadly.

'Ah,' said Mr Bold. 'And Sylvie? Might she read them out to him?'

'No. Neither of them can read,' said Bobby. 'They're wild foxes, remember. They've never needed to learn to read.'

Mr Bold blew out his cheeks with frustration. 'So, I've rather wasted my time then,' he said.

'Not really,' said Mrs Bold brightly. 'The twins enjoyed your posters, and I'm sure Mr McNumpty and everyone else will too. Just, er, not Mossy.'

'Yes, but Mossy is the bully in this house. That was the whole point. To try and educate him,' said Mr Bold despondently. And he began to pull down the posters and signs. Mrs Bold and the twins helped him and then they all had breakfast together.

Suddenly Mrs Bold cried out: 'I've got it!'

'Got what?' asked Mr Bold, somewhat alarmed.

'I've got the answer,' said Mrs Bold excitedly, throwing her toast down on the plate.

'Remember that meeting we had at the Binghams'? When everyone was talking about how to get rid of foxes? Well someone said foxes hate lion poo, remember?'

'Yes, that's right,' replied Fred. 'But how does that help? We don't know any lions.'

'Ah,' said Amelia, raising her paw. 'But we know a lion's cousin. A cougar. Remember?'

'Oh yes, Bertha, our cougar friend who runs the tea rooms down in Cornwall.'

'Precisely. Well maybe whatever it is about lion poo that foxes can't stand must surely apply to cougar poo as well. I'm sure Bertha wouldn't mind helping us.'

So Mrs Bold dialled a number and waited a moment.

'Ah, Bertha! It's Amelia Bold. I trust you're keeping well? I wonder if you might be able to help us out. A rather delicate matter . . . I'm after your poo.'

And so, the next day a package arrived for Mrs Bold, labelled 'Handle With Care'. Inside was a Tupperware container, and inside the container was a generous donation of

Bertha's number twos.

Dear Amelia,

Hope this does the trick and you're soon shot of that pesky fox! Love to all, your friend,

Bertha.

'Bless her!' said Mrs Bold.

'That's what friends are for!' commented Mr Bold.

'So how is it going to work?' asked Betty.

'We'll wait until Mossy is asleep in his den, then just chuck the poo in, I suppose. And we'll leave the front door open. With any luck Mossy will shoot out the den in horror, down the stairs and out. Gone for ever!'

'And good riddance!' muttered Uncle Tony.

'But what about Sylvie?' asked Bobby.

'Sylvie no like poo poo,' pointed out Miranda. 'Sylvie run away too. Big shame!'

'Well,' said Mrs Bold, 'after breakfast I'll ask Sylvie to help me with some new hats. Mossy will have gone back to bed as he always does. We'll wait ten minutes, then we strike.'

'Excellent plan of action,' said Mr McNumpty, who had been listening intently. 'Top notch. Thought of everything.'

'Right,' said Mr Bold. 'Tomorrow is the day!'

Chapter 20

In the morning everyone had breakfast as usual – the Bolds first, then Uncle Tony, Mr McNumpty and Miranda, then the students. They all tried to act as normally as possible, but there was an air of excitement, as everyone hoped they would soon be rid of the troublesome Mossy.

Finally Mossy and Sylvie arrived. As usual Sylvie ate hardly anything but Mossy was particularly hungry.

'Get me some chorizo tacos and a potato hash

and three fried eggs. Then I'll have cheddar cheese frittatas, cherry tomatoes and thick sliced ham and some all-butter sugar buns.'

'Certainly, Mossy,' said Mr Bold obligingly. 'Won't be two ticks!'

After he'd eaten his way through the mountain of food and demanded more buns and a full-fat yoghurt, Mossy belched loudly and yawned.

'Going to go and sleep it off now?' asked Mrs Bold brightly.

'Yup,' said Mossy. 'C'mon, Sylv.'

'Ah, Sylvie, would you mind helping me for half an hour? I'm making some new hats out of rice pudding and wondered if you'd mind doing some stirring for me?'

'Certainly, Amelia,' said the vixen. 'Happy to help.'

'Laterz,' muttered Mossy, giving his tummy a rub, then he left the kitchen without so much as a thank you, and went back to his den.

'Listen, Sylvie,' whispered Mrs Bold. 'We're going to try something that will free us, and you, of Mossy.'

'Whatever do you mean?' asked the startled vixen.

'Mossy has to go. He's making everyone unhappy and he's a bully. But I want you to know that you're welcome to stay with us, if you want to.'

'What are you going to do?'

'There's no time to explain now, but you do understand why we're doing this, don't you?'

'I-I think so,' said Sylvie.

'I'm going up!' said Mr Bold, wearing some bright orange rubber gloves and holding the Tupperware box at the ready. Then he added: 'Knock, knock!'

'Who's there?' asked Mrs Bold.

Europe!

Europe who?

Well, that's not very nice!

Mr and Mrs Bold had a nervous laugh at his joke, then Fred pulled himself together. 'Right. You two, stay in here. Wish me luck!'

After opening the front door wide, Mr Bold crept up the stairs. He paused on the landing and listened to the loud snoring coming from inside the fox den, then opened the Tupperware box. He sniffed at the contents then wrinkled his snout. 'Disgusting!' he thought to himself, then silently counted 'One, two, three . . . !' and threw the contents deep into the den in the direction of the snoring fox, and pressed himself against the wall, ready to watch Mossy's swift exit.

The snoring stopped but nothing happened.

After a tense moment of waiting, Mr Bold looked into the den.

236

'Strange, I thought he'd be out by now,' he muttered, then peered in a little closer. Suddenly a large lump of cougar dung hit him splat on the nose.

'Ugh!' cried Mr Bold. 'That wasn't supposed to happen.'

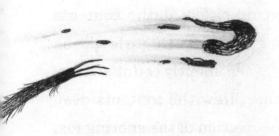

'Trying to scare me away with THAT?' said Mossy's voice. 'You stupid hyena.' And another lump of cougar poo hit Fred, who quickly retreated to the kitchen.

'It didn't work, then?' concluded Mrs Bold, as she wiped her husband's hairy face with a dishcloth.

'Not at all,' said Fred. 'Mossy is still up there, settling back down for his nap. I just got covered in the stuff for my trouble.'

'What was it?' asked Sylvie, her nose twitching.

'Cougar poo. I thought foxes hated the smell and that Mossy would run in terror from our house and we'd be free.'

Sylvie shook her head. 'Lion poo, yes. Terrifies us. Cougar poo, no. Doesn't bother us in the slightest.'

'Ah!' said Mrs Bold. Then she began to laugh. 'It is quite funny though. My Fred covered in poo!'

So of course Fred laughed too. Eventually even Sylvie couldn't resist. And after a good laugh, they all felt much better. But the problem of Mossy remained and the Bolds were out of ideas.

Chapter

The next morning was bright and sunny and there was nothing to indicate that it was going to be a day of great upset and tragedy.

After breakfast Minnie came to visit the twins with her little dog, Walter, and the four of them went to play in the garden.

Mr and Mrs Bold were in the lounge giving the students a lesson on hind-leg walking and general deportment. All three had now mastered dressing up in human clothes and talking – more or less.

Craig liked to disguise his ears under a bowler hat and was rather keen on saying 'How dooo yooo dooo?' to everybody.

Walking and manners were proving to be a bit more of a challenge. But, as Mr Bold pointed out, if Uncle Tony had managed to do it, then anyone could. The Bolds thought it would probably soon be time to let them out into the real world and see how they got on.

Mr McNumpty and Uncle Tony were playing dominoes on the kitchen table.

Mossy and Sylvie had retired to their den after breakfast, and as usual weren't expected to be seen again until lunchtime.

Miranda the marmoset monkey was dozing on the windowsill in the bathroom and it was she who spotted the newly repaired Honda pulling up outside 41 Fairfield Road. She had heard about the breakdown, so when she saw the man in his overalls coming up the garden path she scampered downstairs to alert Mr Bold.

'Man come! Honda better!' she squeaked, just as the doorbell rang.

'Ah, thank you, Miranda,' said Mr Bold. Turning to the students, he said, 'I suggest you all practise walking about some more. Try not to waddle too much, Snappy. It makes you look like a goose, which of course you are, but the idea is to disguise the fact. And Craig – less snorting. Miss Paulina, you're doing very well, but young ladies don't usually twitch their whiskers quite as much as you do.'

'Why don't you invite the mechanic in?' suggested Mrs Bold. 'He sounds very nice and it will be a good test for the students. A brief encounter with someone from the outside world.'

'What? Bring him into the lounge?' asked Fred.

'Yes, why not? Everyone ready to meet a proper human?' she asked the class. There

244

was an excited giggle and much nodding from Miss Paulina.

'Yup!' quacked Snappy.

'If it is your wish,' said Miss Paulina.

'Bring it on!' said Craig.

'Jolly good,' said Mr Bold, uncertainly. 'Back in a tick!'

'I'm not sure they're ready,' said a worried Mr Bold to his wife once they were out of earshot. 'But I guess there's only one way to find out . . .'

The doorbell rang again.

'Hurry up!' said Mrs Bold.

'Coming!' called Fred, and seconds later he opened the door to the mechanic.

'Ah, Bert!' said Mr Bold cheerily. 'Do come in.'

'Car all fixed up for you, mate,' said Bert, stepping into the hallway. 'Here's your bill. I've taken ten per cent off for all the laughs you gave me.' He glanced up the stairs and seemed to be sniffing the air for some reason.

'That is so kind of you,' replied Mr Bold. 'Which reminds me . . .'

What did the duck say after he went shopping?

Put it on my bill!

'Ha ha ha!' laughed Bert appreciatively.

Why can't you borrow money from a leprechaun?

Because they're always a little short!

Bert laughed loudly again. Very loudly. 'Oh, you're a tonic, Mr Bold, you really are.'

'Would you like a cup of tea while you're here?' asked Fred. 'Come and wait in the lounge while I put the kettle on.' Mr Bold led the mechanic into the lounge and introduced him to Mrs Bold. 'My lovely wife. And we have some visitors,' he indicated the three students sitting primly in a row on the sofa. 'This is Craig, Miss Paulina and Snappy.'

'Pleased to meet you all,' said Bert, shaking their paws – or in Snappy's case, webbed foot – which he'd disguised in gloves.

'How do you like your tea?' asked Mr Bold. 'One leg or four? I mean lump. Two lumps, not four. Silly me. One lump or two?'

'No sugar, thank you,' said Bert, smiling broadly and taking a seat by the window. Mr Bold went to make the tea and Mrs Bold nodded at the students, encouraging them to practise their conversational skills.

'Nice day for a swim. I mean walk,' said Snappy.

'Er, yes, I suppose so,' said Bert.

'It's otter than you think,' said Miss Paulina, who immediately realised her mistake. 'Hotter, even. Forgive me. Why on earth did I mention an otter?!'

Mrs Bold winced. This was not going well.

'Mmmm. Quite warm out,' said Bert.

'You fix cars for a living?' asked Craig. 'Interesting? Or boar-ing?'

Bert began to giggle. 'I'm sorry,' he said. 'But, you see . . . Oh my . . . it's just that . . .' But his giggles got the better of him and in a few seconds he was quite helpless, throwing his head back and roaring and bellowing with laughter.

⌗

In the kitchen Mr Bold was stirring the tea in the pot when he heard the happy sound of laughter from the lounge.

'They're getting on well, then,' observed Mr McNumpty, looking up from his dominoes.

'Sounds like it!' said Uncle Tony.

'He's a very nice chap,' said Mr Bold. 'Liked all my jokes and enjoys a good laugh.'

'Clearly!' said Mr McNumpty. Now they could hear everyone joining in the laughter, which seemed to be getting more and more raucous.

'Whatever the joke, it sounds like a cracker!' said Mr Bold. 'I think I'd better go and write it down.'

Just then Sylvie appeared in the kitchen, wide-eyed and alarmed.

'Mr Bold?' she said urgently. 'Who is that laughing in the lounge?'

'Sorry if we disturbed you,' said Mr Bold. 'I'll go and ask them to keep the noise down.'

'No, it's not that.' Sylvie shook her head. 'I recognise that laugh . . .'

'Oh, I doubt it, Sylvie. You don't know him. It's just Bert who fixed the car for me.'

This news seemed to make Sylvie feel faint, and she sat down on the kitchen floor. 'Bert? Car mechanic?' she whispered. 'Then it *is*. It's him. It's Mossy's brother, Bert.'

Chapter

Mr McNumpty's jaw dropped open with surprise.

'You mean . . . Bert is a fox?'

'I knew there was something about him,' said Mr Bold. 'I just couldn't quite put my paw on it. And I was so concerned about getting back to cook for Mossy, I didn't really give it much thought.'

'Well, well, well!' Uncle Tony shook his head. 'He's done all right for himself, then.'

'Please,' interrupted Sylvie, still rather dizzy with shock. 'I must speak to him. Would you ask him to meet me in the garden for a private word?' and she staggered out of the back door.

Forgetting all about the promised tea, Mr Bold hurried back to the lounge. The sight that greeted him was not one of civilised strangers making small talk. Far from it. Everyone was on all fours on the lounge carpet, sniffing bums, rubbing snouts and beaks, and behaving very much like animals.

'Oh!' said Mr Bold.

'Bert is a fox!' said Miss Paulina.

'He saw through our disguises almost at once,' laughed Craig.

'He gets a bit tired of being a polite human all the time,' said Mrs Bold. 'He couldn't wait to get down on all fours again!'

'Oh, Mr Bold!' laughed Bert. 'I knew this was a house full of animals the moment I stepped through your front door.' Bert tapped the side of his nose. 'Animal sense of smell, you see! And there was one animal I could smell above all the others. Fox!' He looked intently at Mr Bold. 'And am I right in thinking a certain vixen in particular . . .'

'Sylvie is waiting for you in the garden,' said

Mr Bold. He could tell from the excitement in Bert's eyes that this was to be a reunion he had longed for. 'Come this way.' Despite all his time living as a human and working as a car mechanic, Bert had immediately reverted to his natural fox-like behaviour and although he was still wearing his overalls, he trotted on four feet out of the lounge and raced sleekly down the hall, through the kitchen and out of the door into the garden.

Outside, the twins and Minnie were playing catch. They were so engrossed they hadn't noticed when Sylvie slipped out of the back door and sat expectantly under a large, flowering pink peony.

The leaves of the plant trembled slightly, conveying the nervousness of the vixen concealed beneath.

But when Bert stood on the back doorstep, panting slightly, Bobby noticed him at once and wondered why there was a fox dressed in overalls in their house. It couldn't be Mossy. He was too thin.

The fox's snout twitched and he immediately turned to face the peonies. Suddenly Sylvie emerged and the two foxes came face to face on the garden lawn.

'It can't be!' said Sylvie.

'It is!' answered Bert.

'I thought I'd never see you again,' said Sylvie. 'That you were off living your new life.' The vixen had tears of joy in her eyes. 'How are you?'

'I'm . . . I'm fine . . . I've missed you.'

The two foxes stood inches apart, their wet noses twitching with excitement and glistening in the evening sunshine.

'I didn't expect . . . What are you doing here?' asked Bert.

'The Bolds took us in after Mossy was caught in a trap. We were only supposed to stay for a little while but Mossy likes being waited on by Mr and Mrs Bold.'

'Mossy!' gasped Bert. 'My brother! Is he here? Can I see him?'

Sylvie glanced behind Bert and looked suddenly worried. 'I don't think that's a good idea. He's changed, Bert. He's been so angry since you left. He won't—' she stopped suddenly. 'He's just come out. Behind you.'

Bert tore his eyes away from Sylvie and turned round. There, on the kitchen step, was Mossy.

'Mossy!' cried Bert, bounding up to his brother, tail wagging beneath his overalls. 'It's me! Bert! Hardly recognised you. Gosh, you've put on a few kilos since I last saw you, bro!'

But Mossy's tail didn't wag in response. It stood upright, quivering with uncertainty and the hackles along the ridge of his back rose up.

'You,' he growled quietly. 'What are you doing here?'

'I work in the garage in Hampton Wick. Came to deliver Mr Bold's car,' said Bert cheerfully. 'It's all a wonderful coincidence. Fate!'

261

Mossy's lip curled, revealing his teeth. 'Get out of here. Go back to where you came from.'

'What? Aren't you pleased to see me?' asked Bert, bewildered by his brother's unfriendliness.

'Mossy, be kind! Please!' pleaded Sylvie.

But Mossy jumped off the step and stood between Sylvie and Bert. 'I'll not be kind to a traitor,' he said.

'I'm not a traitor!' objected Bert. 'I'm your brother!'

'You're no brother of mine. You left us, remember? Think you're someone now, do you? Too good to be a fox?' Mossy was getting angrier with every word. 'How dare you waltz in here and start flirting with my Sylvie. You always thought you were better than me. Well, I'll show you!' Suddenly Mossy threw himself at Bert, grabbing hold of his overalls with his teeth, pulling him to the ground.

The twins and Minnie stopped their game and ran inside to get help.

'Mossy! Stop!' shouted Sylvie, but the two foxes were rolling around on the lawn and over the flowerbed in a flurry of fangs, fur and torn fabric. There was nothing Sylvie could do to stop Mossy's aggression, he was out of control, it seemed. As if to illustrate the fact, Mossy howled and screeched like the wild fox he was. Bert tried to defend himself but Mossy was snarling with rage, biting and snapping viciously. Bert was on his back now, and Mossy stood over him, wild-eyed and triumphant.

'Gotcha!' he hissed, then drew back his lips and lunged at Bert, sinking his sharp teeth into Bert's shoulder. Bert gave a screech of bitter pain and slithered out from under Mossy's paws. Hunched and howling, he squeezed himself through a gap in the fence and limped off as fast as his injuries would allow.

Mossy sat panting on the lawn, covered in mud. He turned to glare at Sylvie for a moment.

'Don't even think about going after him,' he commanded. 'Stay where you are! I'll go.' His eyes narrowed. 'And I'll finish what I started.' Mossy headed towards the gap Bert had escaped from, but suddenly Mr McNumpty was there, blocking his way.

'Enough!' said Mr McNumpty. 'Stop this awful fighting at once! He's your brother.'

But Mossy's eyes were still full of fury. 'Get out of my way, you old fool,' he spat. 'Or I'll bite you too.'

'I won't warn you again!' said Nigel. 'This is a happy, civilised household. You can't and won't spoil that for us. You have treated my good friends badly for too long. Not to mention Sylvie. I won't stand by and watch it any more and I will certainly not tolerate fighting.'

'Let me through the fence, or else!' barked Mossy. 'I'm a wild fox and I fight and bite, so there. I hate you and the Bolds and everyone in this house of fake humans.' Mossy was staring at Mr McNumpty's leg, obviously about to bite.

Mr McNumpty knew there was only one thing he could do in the circumstances. He raised himself up to his full grizzly bear height, puffed out his chest and raised his front paws. His jaws opened wider than ever before and a deafening, terrifying roar shook the ground and seemed to go on for ever. Mossy shrank backwards, tail between his legs, eyes

squinting with sudden fear. When he was a few metres away from the suddenly terrifying Mr McNumpty, he turned and ran, bounding down the side of the house and away.

Chapter

23

The whole, awful altercation had lasted less than a minute, and when Mr McNumpty's roar finally finished there was suddenly silence.

Peering out the back door to check it was safe, Mr and Mrs Bold came into the garden with the frightened twins and Minnie behind them. Walter was not only hidden inside her fleece, but buried deep inside the sleeve, quivering.

'It's all right, he's gone,' said Mr McNumpty, tucking his shirt back into his trousers and straightening his tie. 'Sorry about that. But it was necessary in the circumstances.'

'This is all so awful,' said Sylvie. 'Bert ran that way, and Mossy went after him. Mossy is in such a state, who knows what he might do. I never thought he could stoop that low. What if he comes back for me?'

'I doubt Mossy will show his face here again,' said Mr McNumpty. 'Not after all the trouble he's caused.'

'And not after you roared at him,' pointed out Uncle Tony.

'I hope not,' said Sylvie quietly. 'He's gone too far this time.'

'We wanted him to leave, but not like this,' said Mrs Bold.

'And poor Bert is injured. He might need help!' cried Sylvie. 'What will happen if Mossy finds him?'

'Fred, you had better jump in the Honda and go looking for both of them,' suggested Mrs Bold.

'Yes, good idea. Sylvie, you come with me. You'll be able to spot likely hiding places for a fox. And Mr McNumpty too, if you wouldn't mind. In case we need a bit of grizzly bear muscle again. There's no knowing what we'll find. Amelia, you stay here with everyone else. We may be some time.'

So for the next few hours the Honda slowly cruised the streets of Teddington with Mr

271

Bold at the wheel and Mr McNumpty and Sylvie glued to the windows looking intently for any trace of Bert or Mossy, or any likely hiding place. The atmosphere was tense so Mr Bold thought it might be a good time to tell a few jokes.

> Why was the broom late?

> It over-swept!

> How do you make an octopus laugh?

> With ten tickles!

But there was no response from the passengers.

'Tough crowd,' said Mr Bold to himself. 'Try this one . . .'

Why did the clock get called to the headmaster's office?

For tocking too much!

Then, as they drove along the busy Kingston bypass and had almost given up all hope of seeing either fox, Sylvie let out a sudden yelp.

'There! I saw something furry by the side of the road. Stop! Stop!'

Mr Bold couldn't stop right at that moment, but there was a hard shoulder a few metres ahead and he pulled in there.

'You stay in the car, Sylvie. Mr McNumpty and I will investigate,' instructed Mr Bold. But before he could open the car door, Bert, no longer in his overalls, looking dishevelled, suddenly appeared at the window.

'No, don't get out the car, please!' said the distressed fox. 'It's dangerous. And too awful to see. Let me in. I'll come with you and explain.'

'Bert!' exclaimed Sylvie as he got in the back of the car next to her. 'Are you OK?'

'Oh, Sylvie!' said Bert, gently stroking her face. 'I *tried* to stop him running across the road, but he wouldn't listen. He ran straight out and a lorry came and . . .'

'You mean – Mossy is . . .?'

'Yes, I'm sorry, my dear. He was struck by the lorry and he died instantly.'

Sylvie covered her eyes and began to wail. 'Can I see him?' she sobbed.

'I think it would be better if you remembered him as he was,' said Bert. 'The Mossy we knew and loved in Bushy Park.'

'He's right,' said Mr Bold. 'Let's get you home.' And he shook his head in sorrow and pulled back out into the traffic, heading for Fairfield Road.

'Why was he crossing that busy road in the first place?' asked Mr McNumpty.

'He saw me on the other side, and he was still so angry he just wasn't thinking properly. I shouted at him to stop, but . . .'

'He always hated cars,' said Sylvie through her tears. 'His father was killed by one years ago. And of course they carry people around, and he always thought he was smarter than any human being. It's too awful.'

There was shocked silence inside the little Honda as they drove back to Teddington. But as they reached the gates to Bushy Park, Sylvie opened the window and took several deep gulps of air, closing her eyes.

'Would you mind stopping here, Mr Bold?' she asked politely. 'I just need a moment.'

It was dusk now, the sky streaked with pink. Sylvie got out of the car and wandered to the edge of the ferns, which seemed to wave as if beckoning her.

276

Bert followed her. 'Sylvie. Are you all right?'

'There is no reason now why I can't go back to my old life in the park, and live like a proper fox,' she replied.

'But what about me?' asked Bert. 'Could you not come and live with me in Hampton Wick? I have a lovely house . . .'

'I could if that was what I wanted. But it isn't. Living like a human is not for me, Bert,' said Sylvie, looking out across the green ferns. 'This is my home, here.'

'But now Mossy is gone, I thought you and I could find happiness together. My garage business is successful and, well, I love you, Sylvie,' said Bert.

'And I love you too, but I'm not going to live my life doing what another fox wants me to do. I've spent too long in a life I didn't enjoy out of loyalty to Mossy. Now I need to live the life I want to lead. As a wild vixen in the park. My mind is made up,' said Sylvie firmly. 'I don't want the same life that you do.'

Sylvie returned to the car and said goodbye to Mr Bold and Mr McNumpty. 'Please thank Mrs Bold for being my friend. And the twins. Everyone. I shall miss you all a great deal, but I'm not going back to Fairfield Road.'

And Mr Bold, Mr McNumpty and Bert watched as she wandered away into the undergrowth.

Later that night Mr Bold and Mr McNumpty returned to the Kingston bypass with a shovel. When no one was about, they placed Mossy's body in the boot then drove to a quiet grassy spot on Ham Common and buried him.

Then for a few moments, the hyena and the grizzly bear stood in respectful silence over the fox's grave.

And that night the quiet of Bushy Park was disturbed by a pitiful high-pitched wail.

'But where has Sylvie gone?' asked Bobby and Betty. 'Will she be OK?'

'Oh yes,' their mother reassured them. 'Sylvie will be fine, she just needs some time. She is free of Mossy now though. Free to go back to being a real fox again. A fox that doesn't steal things. I know that's what she wanted.'

Chapter

Several months later

All was back to normal at 41 Fairfield Road. The twins were happy and mischievous and the students were progressing well. Mrs Bold's hat stall at Teddington market had been going from strength to strength. Her 'Edible Collection' was even featured in the *Teddington Gazette*. People came from miles around to see and purchase such unique headwear and it was even suggested she might like to open a shop on Teddington High Street. Mrs Bold was very flattered by the idea but decided she'd miss the cheery atmosphere of the market and the other friendly stallholders.

'Besides,' she said. 'I enjoy selling hats on Saturdays and making them on the other days. If I was in a shop every day, I'd run out of hats rather quickly!'

Then, to everyone's astonishment, a photo appeared in a posh glossy fashion magazine of two (minor) royal princesses at a horse race wearing what was unmistakably a matching pair of Mrs Bold's mud bonnets!

The next Saturday the stall was besieged with lots of women in expensive clothes and dark glasses demanding mud bonnets. Dozens of orders were placed.

'Will we have enough mud, though?' pondered Mrs Bold.

'We've got enough mud for a thousand hats, silly!' said Mr Bold.

Can you guess what he was referring to? Where was there lots of earth going spare?

So it was all hands on deck at Number 41 the following week. The twins' job was to carry bucketloads of earth downstairs from Mossy and Sylvie's abandoned den, then Mr Bold poured in water at the kitchen sink and stirred the mud until it was just the right consistency. Uncle Tony and Mr McNumpty

sat at the kitchen table with bowls over their heads and Mrs Bold sloshed the mud on top, while Miranda the marmoset monkey leaped from table to counter scattering feathers on the still-wet bonnets in a tasteful, artistic manner. (Luckily Snappy had recently molted, so there were plenty of feathers around.) Once the mud had set, the bonnets were eased off the bowls and placed on the draining board to await final touches. Dozens of mud bonnets were made ready for the next market day.

'We'll make enough money for another holiday in Cornwall!' declared Mrs Bold.

'Hurrah!' cried the twins.

And then, as if
life couldn't get more
exciting, one morning
Mrs Bold received a very
important-looking envelope with
the crest of Buckingham Palace on it.

She opened it and gave a shriek. 'We've
been invited to a royal garden party!' she said
breathlessly.

'Wow!' said Betty. 'Whatever shall we wear?'

'Hats, of course!' said Bobby.

The big day arrived and the Bolds were
beaming with pride as they lined up outside
41 Fairfield Road to get into the Honda,
which had been given an especially thorough

clean by Mr Bold and the twins that morning.

'Before we go to the Palace, let's take a short diversion through the park,' said Mrs Bold, giving her husband a knowing wink.

'The park? But we mustn't be late for the Palace,' said a concerned Betty.

'There's someone we need to say hello to and thank on the way, that's all,' replied Mrs Bold. 'Stop just here, now we'll all get out and wait for a moment.'

'There's no one here!' said Bobby as they sat quietly in a grassy clearing.

'Hush!' said Mrs Bold. 'Be patient!'

After a few minutes there was a rustling

sound and a face peeped out through the ferns. It was a fox.

'Sylvie!' gasped Betty.

'Hello, everyone,' said Sylvie. 'You all look smart. Where are you off to?'

'We're going to London, to a royal garden party. Those mud bonnets you helped me to make have become all the rage. I just wanted to say thank you and see how you're getting on, after I got your note telling us you had a new den and were happy.'

'Oh, it wasn't me who wrote it,' replied Sylvie. 'I'm a wild fox, remember?'

Sylvie moved over to where the Bolds were sitting and looked over her shoulder. Another fox followed her.

'Bert!' said Mrs Bold. 'It was *you* who wrote the note and popped it through our letterbox! Are you two . . .?'

Bert nodded, 'So glad you could pop by.'

'Yes, we are a couple now,' said Sylvie shyly. 'Bert came to find me after . . .'

'I realised we were meant to be together,' said Bert, gazing lovingly at Sylvie. 'She could never live as a human, and I could never be

happy without her. So I gave everything up and followed my heart. We're living here, where we are happiest, in Bushy Park. And there is something else to tell you,' he added before giving a high-pitched call. A second later a cheeky, adorable little fox cub scampered out of the tall grass and ran to Sylvie, its mother. Then another cub. And another. The three mischievous young cubs peered at the Bolds for a few seconds, their eyes wide with curiosity.

'It's all right,' Sylvie said to them. 'They're friends.'

A few minutes later, protected from prying human eyes by the tall ferns, the fox cubs were climbing all over their new friends, nibbling and tugging at clothes and playing happily, tails wagging.

Everyone laughed and smiled with animal joy.

Eventually Mrs Bold said, 'We really ought to be going. The garden party, remember?'

'Must we?' asked Betty.

'This is much more fun!' said Bobby, as one of the cubs began to chew his newly made hat.

And so the Bolds never made it to the palace. They were having their own party with the foxes.

They were having such a lovely time they didn't notice the change in the weather until heavy drops of rain began to fall.

Perhaps it is just as well they didn't go to Buckingham Palace. The sudden rainstorm took the guests at the royal garden party by surprise too. The two royal princesses, busy chatting to Lord and Lady Someone-or-other and wearing their mud bonnets, were caught in the deluge.

And what happens to a mud bonnet when it gets wet? Yes, that's right. Large brown trickles of wet mud began to drip down the royal faces.

You might think this was a disaster for Mrs Bold, and would spell the end of her hat business. But guess what? Mud is a very well-known restorative face treatment for tired skin. And the next day the princesses were positively glowing with an ethereal beauty they, quite frankly, didn't have before. And so Mrs Bold's hats became even more popular than ever before!

So sometimes, even if things go wrong they do, somehow, go right in the end. Funny how things work out, isn't it? And I do mean FUNNY!

The End

MR BOLD'S JOKES

Why did the pup chase his tail?
He was trying to make ends meet!

What do you do if a pup eats a dictionary?
Take the words out of his mouth!

How do you hide a horse?
Mascarpone!

What's huge and grey and sends people to sleep?
A hypno-potamus!

How do you tell the difference between a pup and a marine biologist?
One wags a tail, the other tags a whale!

Why was the biscuit sad?
Because his mummy was a wafer so long!

How do you approach an angry Welsh cheese?
Caerphilly!

What did the cheese say to himself when he looked in the mirror?
'Halloumi!'

What did the grape say when the fox trod on it?
Nothing. He just let out a little wine!

What did the left eye say to the right eye?
Between you and me, something smells!

How many skunks does it take to make a big stink?
Quite a phew!

What do you get when you cross a parrot with a centipede?
A walkie-talkie!

Why did the chicken cross the playground?
To get to the other slide!

What did the buffalo say to his kid when he dropped him off at school?
'Bison!'

What bird steals soap from the bath?
Robber ducks!

What do you call an alligator in a vest?
An investigator!

Why couldn't the teddy bear finish his dinner?
He was stuffed!

What woke the ghost up in the middle of the night?
Coffin!

Knock Knock!
Who's there?
Ice cream!
Ice cream who?
I scream every time I see a ghost!

Did you hear about the man who slept under a tractor?
He wanted to wake up oily in the morning!

What has four legs and goes 'boo'?
A cow with a cold!

What happens when it rains cats and dogs?
You have to be careful not to step in a poodle!

Did you hear about the man who went to the doctor with rhubarb sticking out of each ear and custard up his nose?
The doctor told him to eat more sensibly!

Why did the woman run round her bed?
Because she was trying to catch up on her sleep!

What do you call a sheep with no legs?
A cloud!

What did the cat say when he lost his money?
'I'm paw!'

What do you get if you cross a llama with a tortoise?
A turtleneck sweater!

What game should you never, ever play with unicorns?
Leapfrog!

What did the big bucket say to the little bucket?
You look a little pail!